The Black Stallion Mystery

by WALTER FARLEY

Cover illustration
by Lydia Rosier

SCHOLASTIC INC.
New York Toronto London Auckland Sydney

For Rosemary

ISBN 0-590-31309-6

13 12 11 10 9 8 7 6 5 4   6 7/8

Contents

1 BLACK FIRE

On Saturday, July 15th, Aqueduct Racecourse's great stands bulged and overflowed, spilling thousands of spectators onto the track's bright green infield. Officials estimated the crowd at more than one hundred thousand, the largest ever to watch a horse race in New York City. Millions more people throughout the country saw the Brooklyn Handicap on television. The number of television viewers had broken all records for an afternoon program.

News film distributors, however, claimed the most stupendous audience of all. They sent prints of the race to foreign theaters and television stations throughout the world. Never had history recorded so many eyes following a horse race.

And, in a far-off country, one who thought endlessly of destruction watched the race with burning eyes.

Fury and wrath had transformed these normally clear eyes into blazing pits of fire. They never left Alec Ramsay and the Black during the race — and they promised death.

By my oath I shall overtake him with my vengeance and destroy him!

The pair of eyes followed the boy and his giant horse to the post, showing no interest in the other two entries. They watched the stallion charge out of the starting gate with Alec Ramsay's chin almost touching the black mane.

Death to him because of what he took from me.

Heart-rending despair and agony replaced the furious storm in the eyes as Alec and the Black flashed past the stands.

A curse on him for his wings of power. But I shall overtake him and destroy him.

The Black swept into the sharp first turn and Alec shortened the reins. Shaking his head, the stallion swerved to the far outside, twisting in an attempt to free himself of the bit.

A wicked hope filled two watching eyes as Alec Ramsay and his horse almost went down.

But the boy kept the black legs driving beneath him and the race went on.

Death to him for his arrogance.

Now the Black was in full flight with Alec Ramsay stretched flat against his broad back. On and on the stallion came, faster and faster, until it seemed that one could hear the whistling wind he created. Brighter and larger his black image grew as he swept around the final turn and bore down upon the two front runners. He caught them near the finish line and all three straining heads bobbed together. A great roar rocked Aqueduct's stands as the Black jumped with marvelous swiftness into the lead and the race ended.

The two eyes staring at the television screen showed more vengeance than ever when Alec Ramsay straightened in his saddle. The facial features, too, quivered with rage.

Death to him for making me what I am!
Death to him before the fall of another moon!

Sunday afternoon, following the big race, the stable area was quiet. A lone visitor walked slowly through the murky veil of heat that enveloped the day. He went along the hoof-marked dirt lanes until he came to a brightly painted green-and-red barn; there he stopped and went inside, ignoring the sign which read:

NO VISITORS EXCEPT
ON STABLE BUSINESS

The visitor sniffed the strong smells of hay and leather, of horses and liniment. He went on, his eyes quick to note the orderliness of the tack trunks and the hanging pails, brooms and rakes, all freshly painted like the barn. Some of the stabled horses stretched their heads over stall doors, expecting him to pat them, but he ignored them. He continued along the corridor until he was within speaking distance of an elderly man who was raking the turf.

"Good afternoon," the visitor said politely.

Caught unprepared, the stableman jumped at the voice behind him, and then said, "Didn't hear you. 'Afternoon, sir."

"I'm looking for Alec Ramsay."

"He's on the other side. This is the Parkslope Stables here."

"I know. The other side, you say?"

"Yes, sir. Just go around the corner. You'll find him there. Black and white stable colors."

"I know that, too. Thank you. Thank you very much."

The visitor turned the corner and his steps came faster as he saw the black tack trunk with the white trim and bold lettering, "HOPEFUL FARM." But the eagerness left his face when he saw the open door and the empty stall inside. He bit his full lower lip in disappointment. Suddenly he heard the sharp blast of a horse. Turning, the man went to a window and looked outside. Then he walked quickly toward the exit. He knew where to go now. It was in the direction of a towering shade tree, beneath which the black stallion was grazing at the end of a long shank.

At the other end of the shank Alec Ramsay was sitting lazily on the ground, saying, "I'd do it if he'd only let me." He was chewing a blade of grass.

Henry Dailey, sitting in a canvas chair tilted against the tree trunk, asked, "If he let you do what?" He didn't bother to remove the battered gray hat from his eyes.

"Braid his forelock."

"Humph," the stocky trainer grunted. "The likes of him's got no use for braids. That's for women an' tame horses an' he knows it."

"Excuse me," the visitor said.

Startled, the boy and trainer turned quickly.

"You're a quiet one now," Henry Dailey said, lifting his hat the better to see their visitor.

"I didn't mean to startle you," the visitor apologized.

"Not important," Henry answered, chuckling. "We startle easy, Alec and I do. It's *him* that's the calm one." He gestured with his chin in the direction of the stallion. The Black was chomping grass in short, tearing bites. "But I wouldn't get any closer to him if you don't want to get kicked," he warned.

"Oh, I don't intend to! I'm closer than I thought I'd ever be *right now* — that is, to him and you, too. I've always just sat in the stands and watched, never dreaming . . . Well, what I mean is that after I saw that wonderful race yesterday I said to myself, 'If it's the last thing I do, I'm going to talk to the men who know *him* best, Alec Ramsay and Henry Dailey! So here I am. It's perfectly all right with the policeman at the gate if you're worrying about how I got in. He gave me this pass."

Henry Dailey smiled at the white paper being waved at him and let the front legs of his chair drop to the ground. "We're not worrying," he said. "Any friend of the Black is welcome 'round here. Besides, after yesterday it's been much too quiet."

The visitor nodded understandingly and then patted the folded newspapers he was carrying under his arm. "All the sports writers in the city must have followed you to the barn," he said. "I've read every word they wrote."

"They meant well," Henry said, turning to look at the grazing horse. As the reporters had written, there wasn't a mark on the Black to indicate he'd been in the most grueling race of his life. The heavy leaden weights put in his saddle pad by the track handicapper hadn't broken him down. He had the growth and courage to carry such a burden. His sinews were as strong and resilient as steel wires. He'd run free and his muscles had been strengthened for it. His hide was tough and clean and satin-smooth, whipped by rains and wind, warmed dry by many suns. He was arrogant, yes. Yet despite his arrogance he responded to the light touch of kindness and understanding which Alec gave him.

"The tame horse doesn't step on this earth that can run with the Black," the visitor said. "I saw him when he first raced . . . that year in Chicago."

Alec turned to the visitor, studying him quietly before saying, "He'd been a killer of horses. It was instinct that made him fight that day. He's come a long way since then."

"You got him to go on," the visitor said, admiration in his eyes and voice. "You made him race."

"I *asked* him," Alec corrected, turning back to his horse. "One doesn't *make* him do anything."

"I'd like to know more," the visitor said, almost impatient now. "What's he like personally? The little things, I mean, those that don't get in the papers."

Henry laughed. "That's a big order when you're talking about the most publicized race horse in the whole wide world."

Alec Ramsay got to his feet. "Not so big, Henry. I think I know what the man means."

Henry saw the strong blue light in Alec's eyes. It was the look that was always there when he talked of his horse.

"He snores," Alec said, smiling at their visitor. "Sometimes so loud we can't sleep at all, not if we're near him and we usually are, here at the track. At the farm it's a lot better, because the stallion barn is a good distance from the house and we have solid oak barn doors."

Alec turned to the Black, his hand tracing the multitude of veins that stood out beneath the velvet-soft neck.

"Yes," the visitor said gratefully, "that's what I meant."

Alec went on, "He dreams, too. He'll move his legs and sometimes even his tail while he's sleeping. Often, too, he'll snort. I believe he thinks he's racing or at least running, for he dreams most of all the night following a race."

"Last night it was awful," Henry interrupted. "I went runnin' into his stall thinkin' he was dyin' or tearin' the place apart. Instead I found Alec tryin' to tell him the Brooklyn was already over an' he'd won it."

"So that's the way it goes with us," Alec said. "Nothing ever dull or very quiet for long."

"It sounds that way," the visitor offered. "Please go on."

Henry spoke before Alec could continue. "I'm afraid we'll have to cut this short, Mister. It's four-thirty and time for our horse to be fed."

"He's a terrific eater," Alec added. "He takes three meals a day. Six quarts of oats, four whole and two crushed. Maybe thirty pounds of hay, too, special from the farm — timothy and a little clover thrown in for dessert. And sometimes I give him a salad for good measure — lettuce with a little endive, romaine, and leaves of the chicory plant. He likes it a lot."

The visitor nodded eagerly, hoping Alec would go on, but Henry was already on his feet and bringing the session to a close.

"Here's what you want to remember even if you forget all the rest he's told you," the trainer said quietly. "Him and his horse have woven a spell around each other that no one in this business can understand, much less break. Just as wonderful as Alec's love for the Black is his love for Alec. It's as simple as that and it's the only reason we're here talkin' about a great race horse. If it wasn't for Alec the Black would be unraceable. Now he gets mad only when Alec leaves without him.

"On the other hand," Henry went on, even more seriously than before, "Alec wouldn't be the rider he is without the Black. On other horses I can fault him. But not on the Black. Alec grows there an' he knows it. So does his horse. They're for each other and each other alone. You're not goin' to see the likes of it again, Mister. Mark my words. Neither you nor me nor anyone else."

"Just one more thing, please," the visitor called after Henry. "What do you think was their best race?"

Henry stopped and turned. "I always like the last one best, and yesterday's was a thumper."

"It was reported in the newspapers," the visitor went on, doggedly following Alec and Henry into the barn, "that you're planning to ship the Black to Europe for racing there. Is that true?"

"It depends on what paper you read," Henry chuckled. "Some say we're goin', others say not. Actually what I told the reporters was that we're interested. It's a possibility but that's all. There are many good reasons why it would be wise to go and just as many good ones for stayin' home."

They had reached the Black's stall and Henry said, "We have work to do now, Mister, but we want to thank you for comin' around. Always glad to see old friends of the Black."

"Thank *you*," the visitor said, "and I do hope you decide to take him to Europe. It would make exciting reading, *very* exciting."

"It could at that," Henry agreed, going into the stall. He stood in the corner, ankle-deep in the straw bedding, watching Alec wipe the Black with a soft cloth. "It's nice havin' such people come around," he told the boy. "I mean people who think more of a horse than just what they see on the track."

"Yes," Alec answered, without a pause in his work, "it is. But did you notice his eyes, Henry? They were clear as crystal. Sometimes I thought I could even see myself in them."

"No," Henry replied, "I didn't notice. I guess I got eyes only for horses."

2 BLACK GOLD

The famous trainer and rider stood quietly together in the stall, the Black snorting and push-
ing his soft nose against Alec's neck.

"Henry," Alec asked his friend, "how serious
were you . . . are you . . . about taking him to
Europe?"

"So-so," the trainer answered.

"How serious is that?"

"He couldn't go without you," Henry said
quietly.

"No."

"And you want to get back to the farm."

They said nothing more but each knew what
the other was thinking.

He's at his best. It's a pity to take him home now.

Henry said, "Whether we go to Europe or not isn't important. What we got to decide is, do we keep him like he is or do we let him down?"

"He loves to race," Alec said, "even yesterday with all that weight on his back."

"After yesterday," Henry said glumly, "the handicappers will put more lead on him than ever. One of these Saturdays they might break him down."

"Even in Europe?"

"I imagine so. It might be a little better for us over there but not enough to warrant the trip unless we got some other good reason for goin'."

They left the stall and went into the tack room.

"Then I guess the answer is to go home," Alec said, throwing a brush into the trunk. "I'll feed him."

Henry picked up a horse magazine and thumbed through it. "Here's a funny one, Alec. Listen to this: *Three yearlings arrived at New York International Airport from Spain on Wednesday. They are owned by Angel Rafael González and are the first consignment of horses from abroad to be received by John*

13

Hudson, agent. They are to be sold at the Sara-toga (N.Y.) Sales."

Henry glanced at Alec to see if the boy was listening and then read the concluding sentence: *"The yearlings will be at John Hudson's farm on Long Island until shortly before the Sales."*

Alec kept on with his packing. "What's so funny about that, Henry? More yearlings from abroad are being sent over here every year."

"I know," Henry said patiently. "Foreign breeders are after the same money we are. They're providin' a lot of competition, too, because many American farms need new bloodlines and buyers have found a good source in England and France. But you didn't get my point. These three yearlings are from *Spain*."

"What's so special about that?" Alec wanted to know.

"Just that I never thought of it as horse racin' country," Henry answered. "I don't think I'm alone, either. That's the land of the pure-bred fighting bull, not the pure-bred race horse. Wonder how John Hudson ever got mixed up with that consignment?"

"Why don't you ask him?" Alec quipped. "The magazine says they're at his farm and that's just over in Westbury. It's Sunday and he'll be home. So will the yearlings. Maybe they're a better lot than you think they are. Why don't you find out?"

"Got better things to do than that," Henry grumbled.

"Such as griping about weights and handicappers, or going home?" Alec asked, smiling. "It'd do you good to get away for a little while. Also, our business is selling horses as well as racing them. Go see what our competition is like."

"Hummph," Henry grunted. "Horses from Spain aren't goin' to worry the Black's colts none. Still, I can't understand why John Hudson of all good agents should — "

"Get goin', Henry. You know you'd like to see them," Alec prodded.

"Not unless you come along too. You need a breather same as I do. You haven't left this barn since yesterday."

"Sure I'd go, but what about *him?*" Alec asked, nodding in the direction of the Black's stall.

"We'll feed him an' lock up. Slim will keep an eye on him. Another horse won't bother Slim none."

Alec nodded thoughtfully. "It won't take long to get over there and back. Okay, Henry."

A short while later Hopeful Farm's small

van, driven by Henry, rocked wildly down a dirt lane.

"I'm sure glad you don't drive this way with horses in the back," Alec commented.

"Of course not," Henry growled. "What do you take me for — a hack?" He stepped harder on the accelerator.

The low barns of John Hudson's farm suddenly appeared around a bend in the lane and Henry slowed down. "Got to be careful now," he said. "Don't want to scare any young horses."

"There are three out in that paddock just beyond," Alec said, squinting in the bright glare of the setting sun. "Can't be sure, but they look like yearlings from here."

"I'm sure they are," Henry said. "John's cleared his barns, gettin' ready for the young stock he'll take to the Sales. Those yearlings must be the ones from Spain. A couple minutes now and we'll get a good look at them."

Slower and slower turned the wheels of the van. The road was empty and there was a peaceful late-Sunday quietness to John Hudson's farm. Even the yearlings in the big paddock were still. They stood together not far from the fence, their heads up and eyes sharp.

Inside the cab Henry's body suddenly stiffened against the back of his seat as if for support after a staggering blow. His hands shook and he sought to steady them by gripping the wheel even harder. Beside him Alec's face was as pale as his own.

"It couldn't be," Henry said hoarsely. "It's not possible."

"But it is," Alec said. "Except for color and size they're models of him. *They're the Black all over again!*"

When Alec and Henry climbed the paddock fence, the yearlings moved toward them rather than away from them. There was no doubt that the colts had been well handled, but the two horsemen weren't interested in the yearlings' stable manners. Only the glistening bodies held their attention and the two men missed nothing. Two of the yearlings were dark brown, almost black, and the third was a golden-yellow chestnut.

Henry said, "Tell me what I'm seein' and I won't believe you."

Alec answered, "They're everything we've tried to breed . . . and haven't."

Never had the Black sired such models of himself as these three colts from Spain. They made a picture worthy of a great painter. Even then it is doubtful if a master could have caught their fineness of features and form.

The yearlings raised their heads high, eyes

alert. There was a slight movement of a bird directly to their rear and they seemed aware of it without moving their heads.

Henry said, "Like *him* they don't miss much."

Alec said nothing. Nor did he follow Henry as the trainer walked around the yearlings. In all the breeding they'd done at Hopeful Farm no colt or filly had yet inherited the absolute refinement of the Black's head. Alec had taken it for granted, as many horsemen did, that when there is a mixture of blood the head of the newborn colt or filly is almost always the same as that of the less beautiful type. Where then could these colts have come from in Spain? Who owned them and, even more important, what was their breeding?

Alec again studied their dish-faced profiles, with the wide foreheads bulging like shields between their eyes and ears and running part way down the nasal bone. Here could be seen the same concave hollowness as in the Black. Their nostrils, too, were his — long and delicate. Their muzzles were so small Alec could have cupped each one in his hand. The ears were tiny and delicate, pointing inwards, and now that they were pricked up, almost touching at the tips.

Henry said, "Look over here, Alec, an' get away from their heads. You don't ride *heads*."

Alec obeyed the trainer and Henry continued, "The lines of the shoulder and quarters are his. So are the hocks."

"And the fetlocks and pasterns," Alec added.

"No," Henry disagreed, "not quite. They're almost too delicate an' not to my liking. But they're goin' to be big horses and nobody'll know it until they stand beside 'em. It's amazing that..." Henry's eyes left the horses for the house beyond.

"John could tell us who bred them," Alec suggested.

"More important is who *sired* them," Henry answered. "A stallion that can stamp his get to look almost like our horse could be mighty valuable. In fact it's almost like . . . well, what I mean is . . ." He stopped and their eyes met.

Alec said, "It couldn't be the Black's sire, Henry. You know that as well as I do. He's dead."

"A lot of people are goin' to wonder about that when they see these colts in the ring at Saratoga," said Henry. "And whoever the sire is they'll be after him fast." The trainer shifted uneasily on his big feet. "Where's John, anyway?" he growled. "Anyone could walk off with these colts right under his nose. John!" he shouted. "Hey, John! You home?"

A few minutes later a man as short and bowlegged as Henry came out of the house. When he had reached them, Henry said with feigned lightness, "Hello, John. We were hopin' you'd be at home. Nothin' important, though. Just lookin' at your stock for Saratoga. Got anything else we can look at?"

John Hudson had an enormous nose and he brushed it as if to hide a wide smile. Henry had walked behind the colts and was shaking his head in disapproval.

"Do they always stand like that?" he asked. "Pull 'em up a little, Alec."

It was then that John Hudson laughed out loud. "Who are you trying to kid, Henry? You never saw better legged colts. And you also know what they'll bring in the ring!"

Henry shrugged his shoulders.

"Don't give me that offhanded stuff either," the agent said. "You're as surprised as I was when I first saw them. They're carbon copies of the Black and worth their weight in gold. I figured I'd be seein' you the moment you heard about them. But I didn't expect it to be so soon."

Henry moved from behind the horses. "Okay, John, you win. I don't know what I was tryin' to prove anyway. Matter of habit, I guess. Now, these colts. Where'd you get 'em?"

"Spain."

"That's a big country, John. We're old friends, remember?"

"Sure, Henry."

"I'm lucky to be the first here."

"I know that, Henry."

"Who sent them to you?"

The agent ran his hand down the long neck of the chestnut colt. "A gentleman by the name of Don Angel Rafael González," he answered.

"A friend of yours?"

"Nope. Never even heard of him before."

"Did he contact you himself?"

John Hudson nodded. "By letter first. Then he flew them in. His own plane, too, a big cargo job with a private crew. There was money in it. For me, too, when I saw the yearlings come out of it." The agent smiled.

"John . . ."

"Yes, Henry?"

"Of course he turned over the necessary registration papers to you."

"Of course. How else could I sell them?"

"May I see them?"

"They're in the house."

"All three sired by the same stallion?" Henry asked anxiously.

"You didn't have to ask that, but the answer is yes. His name is El Dorado."

"Does this González fellow have him?"

"He said so." John Hudson smiled. "I believe you'd like González, Henry. He seemed to know all about you an' the Black an' Alec."

"Did he give you the impression he might part with this El Dorado?"

"No, but I don't think he'd turn a good price down. He seems to live pretty high and was interested in last year's sales figures. I guess he's something of a playboy although you'd hardly know it to look at him. He's very big and rather ugly — except for his eyes, that is. They're black and piercing like an eagle's. They never seem to leave you. But somehow they don't make you uncomfortable."

"I'm not interested," Henry said, walking toward the horses. "But I would like to see those papers if you don't mind, John."

Later, on the way back to their barn, Henry said to Alec, "If we're smart we'll do something."

"About El Dorado?"

"Of course. I don't know if his colts will run the way they look but they could. We ought to try to buy El Dorado before another breeder does."

"But that isn't all you're thinking about, is it, Henry?" Alec asked quietly.

"No."

"Maybe the Black's sire isn't dead after all.

Isn't that it? Desert Arabs don't always keep written pedigrees, and names can be changed."

Henry nodded. "We'd better find out before somebody else does," he said. "Since we were thinkin' of goin' to Europe anyway, we'd better make Spain our first stop."

3 BLACK ANGEL

The Trans-Ocean cargo plane crossed the Atlantic at altitudes of fifteen to twenty thousand feet, but because of the pressurized cabin its occupants felt no discomfort. Even the occasional bump that marred a flight's smoothness was no different from the ones they had felt a few hours before on the ground. The cargo was mixed — eighteen dogs, four calves, three goats, and one horse. The horse was the Black and with him was Alec Ramsay.

The tall stallion stood in a specially built traveling stall furnished by the airline. It was very strong, the stout wood being reinforced by metal. Inside, it was lined with straw and sack padding so there was no danger of the horse's hurting himself if he kicked or pawed.

Alec had been watchful for any signs of restlessness during the trip but the Black had been quiet. His main interest was watching the other animals in their boxes. Even the almost incessant barking of the dogs hadn't seemed to bother him. So Henry had been right, Alec mused . . . the Black's unfamiliar traveling companions had been more of a comfort to him than a trial. It was a good thing, for they'd had no choice but to take the first air freighter they could get if they wanted to reach Angel Rafael González before other breeders did so.

Three days had passed since Alec and Henry had seen the yearlings at John Hudson's. Within two more days the colts would be taken to Saratoga, where almost every horseman in the country would see them.

Henry hadn't dawdled. He'd used every connection and pulled every string he knew. Passports had been secured within a day. The Spanish Consul in New York was only too happy to cooperate in every way possible, hoping Alec and Henry would see fit "to race the great Black at the *Hipodromo de Madrid*." There had also been a series of cables between Henry and Angel González, with the trainer requesting that they be shown El Dorado.

González had been most gracious and eager to welcome "such famous horsemen whose interest in El Dorado and his colts was very gratifying." He would be happy to have them as his guests for as long as they cared to stay in Spain.

Everything had worked out very well, Alec thought, almost *too* well. He was always wary when pieces fell into a pattern with so little trouble. He shrugged his shoulders and stood up. "That's only because Henry and I have had to work hard for everything we have. We'll never get used to people doing favors for us. How about *you*?" he asked the Black aloud.

The horse glanced his way but turned quickly back to the dogs. He snorted at them and for a moment their barking stopped, only to begin again louder than ever. The attendant in charge tried unsuccessfully to quiet them, and then went back to reading his paperback.

Alec reached over the high sides of the stall to rub the Black's neck. His coat had a rich glow, almost as if it had been rubbed with olive oil, as was often done with show horses before they entered the ring. No need to do that to the Black. His shining coat reflected his good condition and health.

Alec glanced at the cabin door leading into the pilots' compartment, and wondered how much longer Henry would remain up there. He was hoping to get more information about González from the crew, one of whom was Spanish.

A little later Henry returned, taking a seat beside Alec. "Not much," he said. "This González is a gentleman rancher, raisin' fighting bulls mostly. The Spaniard up there was surprised to learn he had race horses. Said his countrymen never have been very much interested in horse racin' even though there's a track in Madrid. Their taste runs more to the bulls. Racin' one horse against another is too tame for them." Henry chuckled. "That's a laugh," he added.

Alec said, "It's a cinch they've never stood on the rail near the first turn."

"No," Henry agreed quietly, "they haven't." His tone tightened. "Anyway, no one up there knew anything about El Dorado."

"And we're crossing an ocean to see him," Alec said. "It's a long jump just to get a look at a stallion."

"Not so long. Think of Abu Ishak going halfway around the world to look at the Black when he learned you had a horse that might be the one he'd lost."

Alec nodded his head, thinking again of the Arab chieftain who had befriended him and changed the course of his life by bequeathing the Black to him.

Henry stood up. "Say, don't these dogs ever shut up?"

"It doesn't seem to be bothering him any."

"It better not or there'd be trouble."

Alec nodded. He had been watching the Black's eyes and he knew there was nothing to be concerned about. The light that flickered and blazed in those eyes when his horse became excited or angry wasn't pleasant to see, for then there was nothing fine and noble about the Black. He fought with fury, knowing no master, no love. At such times nothing remained but his wild desert instinct to kill.

The plane dropped suddenly and sickeningly. The air remained rough and Henry said, "We must be coming in. They said it'd be no more than another hour before landing."

Alec looked out the window into the grayness of a heavy cloud bank. It was mid-afternoon and he hoped it would be clear below.

The big plane dropped into sunlight and Alec could see mountains and swift-flowing white streams tumbling down green hills. Just beyond, however, the landscape changed dramatically from lushness to brown, thirsty plains as golden and tawny as the desert. The treeless land stretched for miles upon miles in the bright sunlight. But soon this, too, passed beneath the swift wings of the plane.

The waterless landscape gave way to more

streams and deep, dark rivers. Villages appeared, dominated by great churches and cathedrals, whose towers rose mastlike into the sky. Row upon row of tall poplars and silver birches separated cultivated fields and small cottages of gray stone. Then this dropped behind and the plane was flying over what seemed to be an endless plain. But it was green and lush like the earlier hills. Great walnut trees grew everywhere, and in their shade grazed large herds of goats and cattle. The great plain was split by many wide streams, where the splashing bodies of young swimmers could be seen.

Lower and lower they flew, the plane braking like a giant sled. Just beyond, the land rose in brown ridges, and here, on the bank of a river, was the city. It climbed the hills in every direction, sprawling and white against the khaki-colored landscape.

The big plane banked sharply, and for the first time during the trip the Black kicked the padding of his stall. Alec spoke to him and rubbed his muzzle.

The brown hills rose on either side of the plane, and Alec could see men at work on the sharply tilted patches of cultivated land. Then they fell behind and the landing strip came up to meet the wheels of the plane. There was a hollow thud of rubber grasping the concrete runway, and the big plane rolled past the airport buildings.

The dogs barked louder than ever and the Black snorted repeatedly. All the animals seemed to know that the plane had landed. Henry went to the window as the plane turned off the runway and taxied toward the largest building.

"There's a flashy yellow convertible out there with a horse trailer attached to it," he said. "That could be our Spanish playboy, all right."

"John Hudson said we'd like him," Alec said, snapping on the Black's lead shank.

"Don't jump to any conclusions," Henry grunted.

A few minutes later Alec led the Black from the plane, quietly and without fanfare. A man who apparently had been waiting for them said, "It is with great pleasure that I welcome you to Spain."

His accent was more British than Spanish. He was everything John Hudson had said of him, big and burly and ugly. Even more impressive than his tree-trunk build was his face. It was cleaved by a long deep scar across his right cheek. Alec found that he was making a great effort not to offend their host by recoiling before it. To avoid embarrassment he faced the man more squarely than before, observing the pallor of his skin, the heavy jowls, and the dark circles beneath his eyes. And such eyes! As John Hudson had said, they appeared to be black and were as piercing as an eagle's. They alone in this deathlike face were vitally alive. Here, Alec decided, was a sick man despite his tremendous, powerful bulk.

Henry shook the man's big hand. "Señor González?"

"Angel, *por favor*," the man corrected, laughing — and surprisingly his voice was not only cordial but deep and strong as well. "Please," he added, "there must not be formality for I feel we have known one another for years. May I call you Henry? And you Alec?"

They nodded in answer, their eyes never leaving the man.

His black hair was short and crew cut. He couldn't have been more than twenty-five years old but one wouldn't have known that from his face. Only the recklessness in his eyes and his wild laugh betrayed his youthfulness.

"Come, my friends," he said, waving a magnificent sombrero, "I am most anxious to take you home. There is nothing to detain us here. I have already arranged for your entry."

González moved toward the yellow convertible, striding with the easy grace of a leopard. Alec walked behind with the Black, wondering what this man in the well-worn, tight leather charro clothes had in store for them.

Suddenly González spoke. "My people, I'm afraid, are not as impressed by the speed of a horse as I am or they would be here to see the Black. But it is just as well for I imagine you have had your fill of such excitement."

González glanced back at the stallion; then his eyes rested on Alec in a flat stare. Seconds ticked by before he shrugged his shoulders and, turning around, continued walking.

The Black eyed the covered trailer scornfully, but did not object when Alec led him inside. He pushed against the padded sides. The stall wasn't much larger than the one on the plane. Alec made certain the ropes holding the stallion were tight enough, and then went to the back seat of the convertible where he could speak to the Black through the small trailer window.

They drove slowly through the outskirts of the city with its rattle and volley of Castilian Spanish. The language was spoken loudly, rapidly, and his high-school Spanish was of no help to Alec at all. Yet the people on the crowded streets were little different from those he'd left behind on the streets of New York. They were just as well dressed, with the same number wearing dark glasses to shield their eyes from a hot summer sun. They stopped before store windows, too, in much the same way

— and Alec guessed that it was no different in modern cities the world over.

Soon, however, they had left the city behind and the convertible and trailer picked up speed. As they rode farther into the country, snatches of the conversation going on in the front seat reached Alec.

"Henry, your picture of Spain is that of a golden legend and a very profitable one — promoted, I might add, by our State Tourist Department in Madrid," González said, laughing. "Actually, your picture of the Spanish dancer lifting up her arms with castanet in hand and tapping out a *taconeado* with her feet is no more typical of Spain than a glamorous Hollywood movie set is of your country."

They passed mud-colored villages with great, vast churches dominating the scene. Over long distances stretched the road, and finally they turned off into a lane that led to a wide river. A glorious summer coolness filled the air. The area was thick with trees, and irrigation ditches ran from the deep, dark river into the meadows.

González brought the car to a stop before a curved, black iron gateway. A sign hung from it, reading:

> *Donde los toros son bravos*
> *Los Caballos corredores . . .*

" 'Where bulls are brave and horses swift
...' " González translated. "Welcome, friends, to
my home and yours."

"Speaking of horses — " Henry began, only
to be interrupted by their smiling host.

"First," González said, "let us look at the
bulls. See them over there, my friend. Seldom
do they graze so close."

The car was moving slowly, and behind a
walled pasture on one side of the road the bulls
grazed in ponderous silhouette against the late
afternoon sky.

"Do not make the mistake of thinking they
are like those you left behind in your country,"
the man said quietly but with great seriousness.
"They are *Los Toros Bravos*, The Brave Bulls,
whose ancestors in ancient days ran wild. They
are fast and bold and persistent in their attack
on anything outside their own herd. A month-
old calf, if separated, will attack a human being
on sight. The instinct to run away, to escape,
does not exist in our fighting bulls."

Henry said, "It must not make for easy traveling around your ranch."

"No, it is not easy. That's why our horses
must be swift."

"Getting back to those horses . . ." Henry
tried again.

But the man had turned away and once more

34

was watching the bulls in the distance. "I realize that it is difficult for you to understand how we feel about our bulls," he said. "We have bred for strength and courage and ferocity in our *toro bravo* as others have bred cattle for the maximum quantity of milk or beef or," he turned to face Henry, "as you have bred horses for speed and stamina."

Now that González had turned in his seat, Alec could see his profile again. He found it easier to listen to Angel Rafael González than to look at him. It wasn't going to be easy to be courteous and polite, to look at their host without flinching before his unnatural ugliness.

"I'm very much interested in seeing your El Dorado," Henry said.

Alec thought he caught a nervous twitching of the man's cheeks. "Tomorrow will be time enough, Henry. He is in pasture."

"We have a good hour before dark," Henry suggested. "Wouldn't it give us enough time?"

Again Alec thought he perceived the nervous tic just below the eye and directly above the deep running scar.

"It will take more than an hour to make you comfortable in my home," González said graciously, but with great finality. He glanced across the fields. "However, you can see him in his paddock from here. Look beyond where the bulls graze."

Far in the distance and separated from the herd by another stone wall, Alec could just make out the figure of a running horse and his band of mares and colts. He watched the horse until the car started again and then he turned back to González. The man's hat cord was drawn tight, cutting into the flesh of his heavy jowls.

Alec waited until an immense house rose into view behind a towering white wall before asking, "Did you breed and raise El Dorado?"

There was a moment's hesitation and this time there was no doubt of the nervous tic high on González' right cheek. The muscular contraction almost closed the man's eye.

"No," González said finally, "he was the gift of an old school friend who does not live in Spain."

"Would you mind telling me the name of the country?" Alec asked cautiously, for it was apparent that his host was not pleased with his prying.

The golden sombrero dipped forward. "Arabia. El Dorado is desert bred." The man's words came sharply and it was plain this particular conversation had come to an end.

Alec didn't care. He'd found out what he wanted to know. He tried to still his mounting excitement. *Was it possible that the sire of the Black was alive and that he had just seen him?*

4   BLACK BULLS

Don Angel Rafael González did not bring the car to a stop before the arched courtyard entrance of the big house. Instead he drove around it, going very slowly and carefully avoiding the crowd that suddenly emerged from nowhere.

Several old women carrying huge clay bowls of food moved among big-hatted men. From a building that must have been the kitchen came the smell of wood smoke and sizzling hot beef. The men doffed their straw hats to González and shouted at the children and barking dogs to clear the way for the moving car.

González said, "First we shall see your horse

rubbed down and fed and bedded safe in a stall with clean straw."

"Do you have any enclosure in which we could turn him loose for a few minutes?" Alec asked. "I like to turn him out while he's still tired from traveling. That way he gets used to his new surroundings without being too playful."

González nodded. "I have one such ring big enough for him to run in without getting hurt."

They drove past the stables, leaving behind the smell of wood smoke. In its place the balmy air became heavy with the sour fermented odor of silage and grain. They passed the small, dark huts of the ranch hands and then before them rose a high whitewashed wall. A ranch hand rode by, hurrying to his supper and singing while his heels hit his horse's flanks in a soft rhythm. His eyes moved over Alec and Henry in a bold stare but suddenly his tobacco-stained teeth showed in a broad grin of welcome.

As González drove through a gate in the high stone wall the grunt of a bull could be heard. The Black echoed the grunt with a shrill snort.

González said, "There is no reason for concern. The bulls here are penned." The car was moving slowly through a tunnel in the wall.

"Where are we?" Henry asked.

"In my big bull corral," their host explained. "It is here that I train my horses and prepare my bulls for shipment." He continued on through the tunnel and they emerged into a large open ring encircled by four or five ascending rows of concrete seats. He turned the car in the center of the sand ring and then drove back into the tunnel, stopping when the rear door of the trailer was just within the ring.

"There," he said, "now you can turn him loose."

"But how about the bulls?" Alec asked with concern. He could hear their grunts, louder now than before.

"They are in the back pens and feeding," González replied. "I shall show them to you if you like."

"I wasn't thinking of that," Alec said. "There's no danger of their getting into the ring?"

The big man smiled. "Of course not, Alec, or I wouldn't have brought you here. Come, let us turn your horse loose."

The Black backed out from the trailer into the long, slanting, afternoon light. He snorted again, his nostrils widening as he smelled the bulls.

Henry said, "Maybe we should spread out so we can wave him down if he works up too much speed."

40

Alec shook his head. "Let's leave him alone. The smell of the bulls will keep his speed down." He spoke to the stallion and unsnapped the lead shank.

At once the Black moved across the sand, slowly and cautiously. He was alert to every sound the bulls made. He went over to the high wall and circled the ring until he'd reached the trailer again. He flicked a glance at Alec but that was all. His eyes followed the wall and he went on again until he came to the wide red door on the opposite side of the ring. There he stopped and snorted. From within came the loud bellows of the penned bulls.

"He is all horse," González said, "or he would not be so interested in my bulls!" The man turned to Alec. "You see, I value courage more highly than speed."

Alec said nothing. He wanted to turn away but couldn't. He was held by the man's piercing black eyes.

"Did you know that the Arabian horse is the only breed with the courage to face a lion?" González asked.

"No, I didn't."

"Or to face a fighting bull, an opponent every bit as fierce as a lion?"

Alec shook his head, and González went on. "History reports many incidents of wild bulls killing lions and tigers in combat. And seven

41

hundred years before the birth of Christ, men were riding the Arabian horse in the hunt of the wild bull for food."

Henry broke the spell González had cast over Alec by saying, "You sound like you're sorry you were born too late for it."

"In a way I am," the big man answered quietly. "That's why I have mastered the lost art of the mounted hunter. In this ring my horse and I face the fighting bull."

"That's not sport, that's suicide," Henry said.

"Oh, no, Henry," González answered, his eyes more alive than ever. "It's art when done properly. Actually, too, it's practiced every day in a more simple form by my mounted herders. They must use their lances in moving the bulls and cows from one pasture to another. It's very often necessary to bowl over bulls to protect horse and rider."

Alec said, "Except that in this ring you meet the fighting bull separated from his herd."

"Yes, then he is at his fiercest and bravest." González smiled. "It is here that I, too, must have great courage."

"And your horse?" Henry asked. "How does he feel about it?"

"No differently. He must have courage as well. He has been bred and trained for this. He has no fear of the bull unless I should become afraid and then he would sense it quickly. But if that were the case I should not be in here at all."

"Do you have time to change your mind?" Henry asked.

González laughed wildly. "It's plain to see, Henry, that you don't think much of my modern version of wild bull hunting. As a trainer you should, for it is my horse who has the greatest skill of all. Seldom do I need to use the lance to keep the bull from him. He is as swift as a racer, as powerful as a Percheron, as nimble as a polo pony. You must see him at work to appreciate him!"

"I'll take your word for it," Henry said.

"I'd prefer showing him to you," the big man said evenly. "You have come many miles to see him and it is only right that — "

"You mean it's *El Dorado*?"

"Of course. And tomorrow morning I shall ride him into this ring. You will be most pleased with his work."

That night Alec and Henry went to bed in a room so vast that it was the equal of two large-size living rooms back home. Long hand-hewn beams ran from one end of the ceiling to the other and many brightly colored rugs were scattered across the wide floor boards. On the bright green walls were lavishly framed portraits of horses and bulls. Over Alec's bed hung a stuffed bull's head, the polished horns reaching out like two huge grasping arms.

"How'd you like to be in the same ring with him?" Henry threw the question at Alec from across the room.

"I feel that I am," the boy answered uncomfortably, his gaze on the sharply tapered horns which were spread out over his head. To get away from them he turned on his side and looked over at Henry, sprawled out luxuriously on his oversized bed. Henry had closed his eyes. No wonder, Alec thought. A meal such as they'd had would have made anyone sleepy — roast beef and fried shrimp, bacon, omelets and chicken, salad, and caramel custard and fruit. He hadn't eaten as much as Henry.

Alec's gaze traveled on to the embroidered draperies and the richly carved chairs with gilded heads of bulls on the arms and backs. It must cost Angel Rafael González a great deal of money to live — and yet from what he'd told them today he was at his happiest defying death. What other reason would he have to pit his skill and horsemanship against a fighting bull?

Restlessly Alec left his bed and went to one of the open windows. The night was hot and full of spiced scents but he was aware only of the smell of sour silage from the bull pens and of deep grumblings from the bulls. Had he and

Henry found the sire of the Black only to lose him to a bull in the morning?

Without turning from the window Alec said, "Henry, we'll know the moment we see this stallion if he's the sire of the Black or not. Now if he is . . ." But Henry was already in a deep sleep and beginning to snore.

Alec switched out the light but stayed at the window. It wasn't late and he wasn't ready for bed. He wanted to know if El Dorado was the Black's sire *before* tomorrow morning.

Alec dressed quickly without waking Henry. He left the room and went down the wide marble stairs to the patio, where a fountain was splaying water into a pool below. The splashing covered the sound of his feet running across the flagstone floor. He slowed down as he approached the grilled iron gate, and opened and closed it carefully. Now he was free of the house and courtyard. It was pitch-black but soon the moon would be up to help guide him on his way.

He followed the drive until he could make out the main wall in the darkness beyond. As he came closer he wondered if he'd find the entrance gate locked. It wasn't. It swung open easily beneath his touch.

After walking a short distance down the road he came to the pasture fence. He had no trouble climbing it for the stones jutted out, giving him a firm foothold. At the top he hesitated a moment, then dropped down. He was in the pasture where he had seen the big bulls that afternoon.

He was proceeding cautiously when he stopped again, this time turning to look behind him *and listen.* He thought he'd heard the scuff of leather against stone, the same sound he himself had made while climbing the wall. But to his straining ears everything was absolutely quiet and he went on, believing his imagination to be playing tricks with him.

He turned to the east, waiting for the moon to rise and show him his way. A breeze sprang up, rippling the grass at his feet. From the far end of the pasture came the blowing of a bull; another bull answered.

Alec went on, satisfied that the herd was far away. He had nothing to fear from the bulls, and soon he'd find El Dorado behind his walled paddock.

He walked faster, at times breaking into a half run, for he was very anxious to reach the stallion and return to the house. Yet he wasn't taking any chances of being surprised by a lone bull. Such a possibility was very remote, he knew. The herd instinct, as González had mentioned at dinner, was very strong. Only a rogue or an outcast would be grazing alone. Alec's sixth sense, an awareness of the presence of animals even when he could not see them, told him there were not any near by. He listened to the sounds of the bulls in the distance and hurried on.

A few minutes later he came to an abrupt stop, certain he had heard rustling in the grass directly behind him. *The breeze had died.* What had accounted for the sound? Footsteps? Hoofbeats? Man or bull? He could not tell. Sweat trickled down his body as he stared into the darkness, every sense alert.

He thought he heard the sharp intake of a person's breath and the massive movement of a great body on light hoofs. Could there be both man and bull? Or was there nothing at all? The sounds — assuming they were not the product of his imagination — had stilled.

He stood quietly, knowing it was not wise either to walk or to run. In this pasture were no cows or calves but full-grown fighting bulls, as dangerous as any other fierce animals in the world. He'd realized that before climbing the fence. And he had no weapon with which to protect himself.

It was a bull and it was alone, separated from the herd either by a fight with another bull or . . . Had he actually heard footsteps as well? Had someone intentionally separated this lone bull and arranged this meeting?

Alec listened to the movements of the bull.

He could not yet see him. The wild animal was trotting now, coming toward him faster and faster. Alec had no time to run even if he had wanted to. His heart pounded madly but there was no trembling of his hands or body. His muscles were ready. He didn't fool himself into believing that he had the strength and skill to cope with such an adversary. Standing one's ground against an unruly horse or dog was not the same as facing a bull bred for centuries to attack.

Yet the cavemen had managed, going naked and unarmed to hunt this very beast for food, according to González. At least they'd had a club, Alec reminded himself bitterly. He had nothing, nothing but his wits.

Where was the moon? Would its light help or make things worse? The bull had come to a stop in the darkness, seemingly undecided which direction to take. Alec held his breath. The bull blew, whistling through his nostrils. It was different from the Black's whistle — hoarser and more guttural. Alec heard the hoof-beats come closer, then stop again. Perhaps if the moon had not emerged from behind the clouds at that particular moment the bull might have returned to his herd. As it was, the light brightened the pasture and the two looked into each other's eyes, the bull more surprised than Alec.

Less than a hundred feet separated them. The bull was a big one, his neck a tremendous hump of muscle. The animal lowered his head, his great horns pointing menacingly, and pawed the ground. Then he blew again. Alec knew the attack was about to come.

He had no more than a second to wait. Like a black thunderbolt the bull charged, the rush of his great body shaking the earth and stirring up a sudden gust of wind. Alec twisted away to avoid the horns seeking his flesh. There was a quick movement of the bull's head and the tearing of cloth as the tip of a horn ripped Alec's white shirt at the waist. The passing body struck him hard and he fell to the ground.

The monstrous bull was swallowed by the night but before Alec could get to his feet he'd come out of the darkness again. Alec lay flat on his stomach, knowing there was no escape.

The bull lumbered over him, kneading his prone form with hoofs and head. Fortunately the horns struck only the ground on either side of his body. He was butted and bumped by the big head. He could only lie still, praying that if there was no movement from him the bull might stop before the horns pierced his body. He buried his face in the deep pasture grass and suddenly the bull stopped.

Alec waited and held his breath. The bull butted a final time and the tip of a razor-sharp horn caught the back of Alec's neck. Alec felt the blood start to run down his back. He listened to the bull, who was moving away . . . a stride, then another and still another . . . one more and he stopped. *Was he turning back?* Alec raised his head to find out.

A breeze had come up and Alec saw that the bull's eyes were upon his ripped shirt which hung loosely outside his pants. Its fluttering in the wind had attracted the bull's attention. Suddenly the great head lowered and then the beast charged again!

Alec sprang to his knees, tearing part of his shirt off at the same time. He held it in his hands when the bull moved upon him, knowing he had one last chance to avoid the horns. He shook the white cloth, holding it far away from his body . . . *and the bull's eyes and lowered head followed it, thundering past!*

As the tremendous bull slithered by him, Alec jumped to his feet. Now the bull was raging, fighting mad. He charged again and Alec could hardly believe his eyes as the savage horns passed harmlessly through the cloth once more.

Alec pulled off the rest of his shirt to provide a larger target for the bull's attack. Again the head was lowered and the forehoofs pawed the earth in mounting fury. Again the bull charged.

Alec stood still and kept the waving cloth as

far away from his body as possible. The horned head followed the cloth, found it, ripped it, and went past. But this time instead of going on the bull turned, sending grass sods flying into the air. He came back again seeking the waving cloth and Alec barely got it into position before the bull was upon him. A horn tip caught hold of the fleshy part of his lower arm as the big body went past, brushing his own.

The bull didn't attack again immediately. He stood about fifty feet away, breathing a little heavily with his tongue hanging out. His eyes never left the cloth.

Alec lowered the cloth to the ground and the eyes followed it. He moved it to the right and the eyes moved with it. Alec took a step backward and then another, trailing the cloth . . . and always the eyes followed it and not him. The bull moved with him, too tired to charge the cloth just then. Alec backed faster, going in the direction of the stone wall.

Far down the pasture came the snorts and grumblings of other bulls. Alec felt the soft earth of a stream bank sucking at his ankles. All he had to do now would be to trip and fall, and it would be the end.

The bull got ready to charge again and his roar shattered the night. He sniffed the air and twitched his tail. Then he moved forward, his ponderous body starting off clumsily, heavily,

51

then shifting into a canter and finally into a full gallop. Alec shook the white cloth. The bull caught it, ripping it again. He passed by, turning as Alec turned, and came on again. Once more the thunderous body swept by Alec and came to a stop. The bull was becoming tired of charging but his fury was not yet spent.

Alec backed into a wild cactus plant, the razor-like thorns driving deep into his legs. He moved around the plant and went on, knowing he couldn't be too far away from the stone fence but not daring to take his eyes off the bull.

The beast roared and charged once more. This time he did not charge staight through the cloth but hooked his horns to the right, catching the cloth and tearing it from Alec's hands. He butted it on the ground, trampled on it, sliced it with his great horns until it was nothing but shreds. Then he turned away from it and looked at Alec.

The moon disappeared behind the clouds and once more complete darkness enveloped the night. The very earth seemed to tremble with the thunder of the bull's pawing, and Alec wished that he could melt into the night. Suddenly the pawing stopped. The bull blew through his nostrils, breaking the air. Now, Alec knew, the charge would come. He stepped backward ... faster, ever faster.

The barking of dogs suddenly echoed the bull's roar and from near by came the tinkle of cattle bells worn by some of the cows in the pasture across the road. Alec took another hurried step backward. His hand touched the cold stone wall!

He climbed as the bull charged, springing harder and higher than ever before in his life. As his fingertips reached the top of the wall and he began pulling himself up, the air beneath him was splintered by the massive horned head.

Alec dropped down to the ground on the other side of the wall, his wounds bleeding more profusely than ever. But he was thankful to be alive. It was more than he'd counted on.

5 BLACK MARÍA

Above the splash of the water from the patio fountain a rooster crowed. Angel González said, "It's a pity I had to awaken you before the first light but . . ." He shrugged his big shoulders easily and gracefully without finishing the sentence.

"It's not hard for us," Henry said. "Knowing the light of early morning is one of the rewards of working with horses."

"And bulls," González added, smiling. "But come, let us eat so we can be on our way." He stirred the thick black coffee at the bottom of his big cup. "María," he called, "milk, please."

From outdoors came the jingle of spurs and

neighs of horses. The sun reached over the patio wall and fell warmly upon the flagstone terrace. Henry waited for it to enter the open doors and windows of the dining room. Not that he was cold. He just needed a bit of cheering up and the sun might do that for him. He had a feeling something was wrong.

"You say Alec went to his horse before I called you?" his host asked.

"Just a few minutes before. He's an early riser where the Black is concerned."

"It is good to tend one's horse before one's self," the big man said. "Young Alec is to be highly admired."

"He's a horseman," Henry said simply. He toyed with his fried eggs and his gaze swept the huge dining room with its heavy antique furniture and silver plate, its mounted bulls' heads and portraits, the hanging chandelier and marble floors. He longed to be away from this house. It was too rich for his blood, as was Don Angel Rafael González.

A great bulk hovered behind him. "More coffee, Señor?" the servant asked in hesitant English.

"No thanks, María," he said, smiling but not looking up at her. Like everything else in the house María was big, almost as big as González. She was as gracious as he, too — except for her ancient eyes which said, *"Who are you and why do you come here?"*

Alec entered the room and Angel González greeted him while María poured steaming milk into his coffee cup. Henry noted the sudden raising of the old woman's drooping, waxen eyelids. Her eyes disclosed the same resentment they had shown when he entered the room. But her voice did not betray her as she asked Alec graciously, "Would you prefer chocolate, Señor?" Her gray head nodded as if she knew what his answer would be.

Alec said, "Please."

María's voice was too sweet for her age, almost honey sweet, Henry decided. It put his nerves on edge. There was too much bitterness underlying the sweetness. Or was he making too much of all this?

He turned to Alec. The boy's shoulders were hunched forward and his left hand was sunk deep in his pocket. Such table manners weren't typical of Alec. Neither was the turned-up collar of his polo shirt. Henry didn't have to be told that Alec was up in arms about something and trying unsuccessfully not to show it.

"The Black all right?" Henry asked.

"Fine," Alec answered. "I cleaned out his stall . . . that's what took me so long." He removed his left hand from his pocket to take the plate of freshly baked bread which María offered him.

Henry saw the heavily bandaged arm. "What'd you do there?" he asked anxiously.

"It's nothing. A scratch. I got everything I needed from the tack trunk."

"Scratches around a stable are never nothing," Henry said with concern. "You'd better let me look at it."

"It's all right, I tell you," Alec said sharply.

Henry turned back to his eggs. That tone wasn't typical of Alec, either. What was up? This house, this whole setup spelled trouble. Why?

María placed two boiled eggs before Alec, and González said, "Here in Spain we do not eat much breakfast. Coffee is enough for me until lunch."

The big woman scowled, the many wrinkles in her face deepening. "Ahh," she snorted. "You slink into the kitchen all morning to steal cheese and shrimp and bits of bread behind my back!"

González scowled in return. "Stealing, María?" he asked. "You mean I steal food in my own house?"

Her sallow features suddenly softened, becoming almost angelic. Her voice was motherly with a moving sadness. "You are not well. For all of your twenty-six years I have known it and cared for you. You do not eat right or live right!"

"Shh, María," González said nervously. "We have guests. Let us not discuss problems of the health." He smiled but could not control the twitching of his right cheek.

Alec finished his eggs and turned to Henry. The trainer was still toying with his food, removing bits of pimento and olives.

The woman went on, "They might as well know, too, that you are a sick man," she said angrily. "It is *they* who want to see you killed!"

"*María!*" González exclaimed sharply. "*Go to the kitchen!*"

"No," she said quietly. "They should know what they have asked you to do." She walked around the table, nervously straightening the silver bowls and pitchers. She moved in a shuffle, wobbling from side to side on her large flat feet.

Apparently accepting María's refusal to leave the room, González laughed wildly and said, "She worries about the bulls and always has. I get a scratch from a *becerro*, a young bull barely older than a calf, and she has the priest at my bedside!"

Alec glanced at the woman and found her brown eyes upon him. She said accusingly, "If you had not come, he would not enter the ring again. He promised!"

González was snapping his fingers, apparently in rhythm to the woman's voice. If he was doing it to stop her it had no effect.

"If God was not with him, he would have been killed long before this," she said thickly.

"I am as big and strong and brave as a bull, María," the man said lightly. "You know it."

"Strength has nothing to do with it!" she almost shouted. "And by being *big* you are *bigger* for the bull's horns to find!"

"You're being ridiculous," the big man scoffed.

Alec clasped his bad arm. The collar of his shirt felt tight because of the bandage around his neck. He understood only too well what this woman was talking about.

María had cocked her head, birdlike, but her eyes were as hard and cold as flint as she looked upon the man she obviously considered more of a son than an employer.

"You are too emotional to fight the bulls," she said. "Even as a little boy you were too close to everything you tried to do. You *feel* too much. You cannot become emotionally involved with the bulls *or you die.*"

Alec glanced at Angel Rafael González. The big man was no longer snapping his fingers to the woman's words. As he listened to María he was the picture of doom. And although he had silenced his fingers he had no control over the nervous tic below his eye.

"Ten years ago it was racing cars," she accused him. "Later it was planes. Then came the bulls! First you were content to ride with your *vaqueros*, using your herder's lance to tumble young bull calves in moving them from field to field. Soon this, too, bored you. So you separated full-grown bulls from the herd and met them in the ring. Only then were you happy, for you were defying *death*." She was crying when she left the room.

González said with embarrassment, "Ridiculous accusations. It is a wonder that I stand for it. Still," he shrugged his shoulders, "she has been everything to me, as she says, mother and father. But enough of this! Come with me while I prepare for the ring. I have already sent for El Dorado."

They went to his bedroom where he pulled on two pairs of long white cotton stockings beneath his pants and leather *zahones*. He changed his shirt and put on a short leather jacket. Both were soiled and wrinkled.

María entered the room, her eyes dry. "See how fearful of the bulls he is!" she said scornfully. "He will not let me wash a dirty shirt because it is pale with the sand of the bull ring!"

"I fought well in it," González answered matter-of-factly. "Please go, María, and leave us alone." He slipped a gold chain and cross around his neck, ignoring the woman, who hadn't budged. Nervously he unbuttoned his jacket and reached for a cigarette in his shirt pocket. There was no doubt that he was upset regardless of all his brave talk.

By her ridicule, María sought to embarrass him still more and keep him at home. She turned upon Alec and Henry and said shrilly, "He goes because he cannot help himself, yet he is deathly afraid. You have only to look at him to know!"

The big man took a round, wide-rimmed hat from his closet. Like the shirt and jacket it was soiled with the sweat marks of many hours spent with the bulls. "It is no time to flout one's courage," he said quietly, "or, for that matter, one's superstitions." Without looking at María he fingered the thin red chin strap, twirling the hat while he finished his cigarette.

"Of course," he said, glancing at Alec, "it is not so strange that one's heart beats a little faster before such an encounter. My young friend understands what I mean, since he has many times awaited the opening of a starting gate."

The woman laughed loudly. "Your young friend would run for his life if the *toril* gate opened and he saw the bull come charging out of his darkened pen! No, it is not the same at all. Your young friend's heart pounds fast with stimulation, *yours with fear!*"

The big man finished his cigarette and stomped upon it with his boot. "I'm dry," he said. "Get me water — and quickly."

María met his gaze defiantly, then poured a glass of water from a pitcher beside the bed. "You are always dry on such a day. You won't eat for fear of being gored and requiring an operation. But you will drink water, gallons of it."

"That is my business."

"*You* are my business," she answered and there was a sudden softness to her voice. "Please give me peace. Give up this dance of death."

González laughed and the sound of it filled the room, the house. He kicked a booted foot high in the air, pretending to dance. "My herdsmen would laugh to hear you call it so. Every day they ride with the bulls and return safely at night." He reached for her but she flung his hand away.

"Is it not different," she asked softly, "that you are alone with a raging, fighting bull in a small cage?"

"I have my horse and lance," he answered, smiling.

She turned to him, her eyes wet with tears. "You are afraid and yet you go," she said simply.

He shrugged his big shoulders. "Perhaps a little afraid, María, but it will pass quickly. In the ring there is no time for fear." His voice was as soft as hers. "I see I cannot even pretend to be a hero to you, *ever.*"

"You risk your life for nothing."

His arms swept gently around her. "It is not for *nothing*, María. I wish you would come just once to see how beautiful it is. Please come."

She shook her head. "You cannot always win. The bull must have his day, too." She burst out crying and his big arms pressed her close.

"Now, now, María," he said. But she turned tearfully from him and went toward a large crucifix on the far wall. There she knelt before it.

For a moment González watched her, then he turned to Alec and Henry and smiled. "Come, the longer we make the bull wait the angrier he becomes."

Henry couldn't help saying, "Perhaps you're looking forward to all this, but what about your horse? How do you think he feels?"

The big man smiled at Henry's obvious sarcasm. "Come," he said, "I'll be glad to show you."

Alec stared at the man's back. At the other end of the room María would remain at the foot of the crucifix until González returned safely from the ring. Alec looked at her and then followed the two men out the door.

6 BLACK DANCE

As they left the house Henry asked González, "Is the object of this to kill the bull before he kills you?"

"No one gets killed, Henry," the big man answered patiently. "Not the bull nor my horse nor *I*." He shoved his round hat far back on his head, straining the red chin strap which cleaved deeply into his chin. "You must think of this as Art and not Sport. The beauty of it lies in the skill and agility with which my horse avoids the bull's charge. I use my lance only when necessary as is done in the fields."

"And your horse enjoys this?" Henry snorted.

The smile on González' face disappeared. "You do not believe me?" he asked coldly. "As a trainer don't you know it's impossible to train a horse to love cruelty? You will see for yourself how willingly El Dorado faces the bull. He has no fear, having spent most of his life within the shadow of the herd. It is his life just as your horse has been trained to race." He turned from Henry saying, "But you will see all this for yourself. There is no need to discuss it any further."

The sky had clouded and a fresh wind rippled the grass between the house and stableyard. From the private ring came the mutterings of the penned bulls. González cocked his head and eyes in its direction and then glanced skyward — nervously, Alec thought.

The boy's attention quickly left González, however, for silhouetted against the whitewashed wall of the bull ring was El Dorado! A herdsman stood at the head of the black horse, holding a long wooden lance over his shoulder.

Henry had seen the horse too, for he glanced at Alec and each knew what the other was thinking. They were several hundred yards from El Dorado and closing the gap quickly. There was no question in their minds that this was *not* the sire of the yearlings they had seen in America. They would have staked their professional careers upon it.

"Is that El Dorado?" Henry asked suspiciously.

"Of course. There is no other like him in Spain. He is all horse."

They neared the stallion. There was no doubt that his midnight-black body carried a strain of Arabian blood from the highlands of Central Nejd. Alec and Henry had seen enough such horses in Arabia to know. And they knew he would have the courage to stand his ground before lions and tigers as well as bulls. *But El Dorado was no race horse and could have sired none!* His quarters were too huge and his hocks too let down and too far under him. They could picture him crouching upon his heavy muscled hindquarters, ready to leap into the air upon an unsuspecting enemy, or performing some intricate movement of a finished *dressage* horse. They knew he could turn on a dime with the agility and grace of a fine dancer, that every movement would be as quick and sure and wily as a jungle cat's. He had been bred to accomplish such feats and he would have stamped his colts *as his* in one way or another regardless of what mares he was bred to. But to be asked to believe that he could have sired race horses such as the yearlings they had seen was ridiculous! Why was González lying? And if El Dorado hadn't sired the Sales yearlings, what stallion had?

Neither Alec nor Henry asked these questions of the big man. They knew they wouldn't get the truth. They stopped before El Dorado, noting the Arabian head with the enormous purple-brown eyes. His neck was short and bulging with muscle. Quality and courage stood out all over him.

González placed a hand on the heavily muscled hindquarters. "See how eager he is to go, my friends! It is more than a week since he has worked the bulls, and he knows what is at hand." The man's face flushed with the pride he felt in the horse who danced so lightly beneath his hand. Then he mounted.

Alec and Henry stepped back, watching González take the long lance and sling it gracefully over his right shoulder. They could think only of a knight going off in search of a dragon or a Roman gladiator about to enter the Circus Maximus to amuse Julius Caesar.

The big man sat with easy grace in the deep herder's saddle that was strapped snugly over a red-and-yellow blanket. The line made by his back and shoulders reminded Alec of pictures he had seen of centaurs. González oozed confidence, leaving no doubt that he would be bold and persistent in attack.

He burst out laughing at the sight of their sober faces and pushed his round hat forward to a jaunty angle. "You look so worried, my friends," he said, shifting the lance beneath his right arm and letting the blunt end extend several feet in front of El Dorado. "Let me cheer you up!" His heavy stockinged legs bulged beneath the leather of his *zahones* as he sent his mount forward and rode into the ring.

Alec wondered how a person so big could sit so lightly in the saddle. He waited for González to give the signal for the *toril* door to be opened. The big man reached inside his shirt pocket for another cigarette, delaying the moment of decision.

"Do you think he's afraid?" Henry asked.

"No. It would be the end of him if he was," Alec answered.

"Then what's he waiting for?"

"The right moment, I guess. See how he's talking to that black stud with his legs, Henry? He has him right up to the bridle, to the tips of his fingers. You've never seen a horse collected like that!"

"No, I haven't," Henry admitted. "It's not my business to — any more than it is to see a rider sit like he does. It's as if he had an iron rod sewn up the back of his jacket."

They could hear horns scraping now, rattling the wood behind the closed red door. Any second now the bull would come out into this cloudy, overcast day searching for his herd and finding instead a mounted herdsman. They were glad they stood behind the *barrera*, a wooden fence that encircled the ring. They could just see over it.

El Dorado was the picture of restrained energy. He was ready to go, and impatient that the command hadn't come. He began dancing in place, his knees coming up high while his hind legs remained still. He snorted constantly.

Alec thought, *"The final moments are always the longest and hardest."* He felt that his own mouth must be as dry as González' and he wished that he had some water to rinse it out. He smelled the horse manure in the sand and the tobacco smoke from the burning cigarette which González had cast near him. He could smell the bull, too. Wrapping his fingers about the top of the *barrera*, he waited.

The red door swung open and a big black bull rushed into the arena, coming to a stop in the center of the ring. He did not bellow or paw the dust. Slowly he looked around, his great neck muscle swelling and bulging. It was as if he had all the contempt in the world for those who would try his patience by keeping him confined.

Alec took his eyes off the bull to glance at González. The man had not moved a muscle. Was he pondering the wide horn-spread of this bull? The quietness of the ring was filled with peril.

Suddenly the bull bellowed and pawed the sand, flaying it in the air. He turned his wide horns toward the man and horse. Again he became still; then without a snort, gasp, or warning of any kind, he swept into action. He raced across the sand, his wide, branching horns reaching for their target. When they found nothing he skidded to a stop, his horns crashing into the wooden *barrera*. He turned away from the fence, surprised and baffled. Once more he lowered his head and followed the twisting run of the horse.

González had his long herder's lance under his right arm and was ready to use it if necessary. So far the bull hadn't come close enough. He touched El Dorado with his legs and the horse moved forward, his bright eyes upon the black bull who was attacking again.

González touched rein and El Dorado went into a long, loping run, leading the bull to the left. The big man sat very still in his saddle, judging the distance between his horse and the bull and bracing himself in his right stirrup. To avoid the bull's charge by a touch of rein and leg was an art, while resorting to a lance was the work of a herdsman.

He brought El Dorado to a dead stop as the bull lowered his head and charged straight at him. The black horse pivoted swiftly on rigid hind legs as the bull passed a few inches away from him. Riding to the middle of the ring, González stopped El Dorado directly in the heart of the enemy's stronghold. Now more than ever his horse must be alert, for the bull was tricky and had plenty of room in which to maneuver.

The big man's heart pounded a little faster. Perhaps he shouldn't have come to the middle of the ring so soon, he thought. But before he had time to change his mind the black bull charged again. El Dorado jumped as the ivory-smooth horns reached for his underbelly. González used his lance, toppling over the bull.

The big man rode El Dorado to the *barrera,* breathing hard. He was angry, not with the bull or his horse, but with himself. He'd been caught unprepared. He had had to use the pole like a common herder to protect himself and his horse. He must do better!

He took a long, deep breath as the bull charged again. This was a master bull, a *toro de bandera,* one of the best he'd ever raised! Eagerly, González swung his horse around, leading the bull in a crazy, twisting run that brought the beast closer and closer to rider and horse. As the bull tired, González let him come only a hair's-breadth away before avoiding his charge.

Satisfied as he now was with his work, González had another worry on his mind — the weather. He glanced nervously up at the sky, which was still overcast and held the promise of rain. It was not a good omen. Neither was the wind, which began whipping the Spanish flag on the pole at the northern end of the ring. Even as these thoughts ran through his mind, several drops of rain struck his hands and trickled off. The wind ruffled the sand around his mount's hoofs. Soon the footing would be wet and slippery. He'd better not work as close to the bull as before. He called to the bull across the ring, "Whuh-hey! Whuh-hey!"

Yet despite his shrill challenge, the big man nervously unbuttoned the top button of his jacket to touch the gold chain and cross about his neck. He pulled down his old leather hat with the red chin strap as the drops turned into a thinly driving sheet of rain. Then, tightening his legs about El Dorado, he rode forward to meet the bull.

7 BLACK SAND

Behind the *barrera* Alec's gaze shifted uneasily
from the man and horse to the leaden sky and
then back to the bull. The spectacle in the ring
was unlike anything he'd ever seen before and
he wished that it were over. The rain should
have put an end to it, but how could such an
encounter be called off? Who was to tell the
bull that it was over?

Alec watched the beast standing in the center of the ring. He was breathing hard but he
held his head high and his small eyes never left
the man and horse. His lust to kill seemed
greater than ever.

Alec was glad of the strong wooden *barrera*

that shielded him from the bull. How must González feel? He'd seen the big man glance nervously at the sky and touch the gold cross before riding forward. Was González becoming less confident as the bull became wiser in his ways of attack? If so, couldn't he have the *toril* door opened so the bull might leave the ring?

The horse moved toward the bull, his hoof-beats steady and confident. At a touch of rein and leg he jumped nimbly away when the bull charged, turning with the bull as the black beast slid and twisted past him in the sand. Then he kept close to the bull, avoiding the horns by sidestepping and allowing his opponent no distance to charge. Finally he swept around the bull and crossed the arena.

The bull wheeled around after the horse but didn't follow him. Instead, he stood quietly in the center of the ring for several minutes. Then he came on again, his head low and driving. But before his horns could scoop the horse into the air, El Dorado was gone.

The thin rain had turned into a downpour. Once more the bull stood his ground quietly, watching horse and rider with his tail swaying back and forth. When he finally swept into action, he did not charge in a straight line as before. Instead he moved to the left with the horse, the curve of his horns swinging up in a semicircle and missing El Dorado's hindquarters by inches. He was learning to fight in the ring, to go with his target rather than to lower his head and charge blindly by instinct.

Alec glanced at González and saw immediately that the big man was visibly shaken by his narrow escape. Alec himself was sickened by the whole business. The duel had become almost too terrible to watch and he wanted to leave, but these final desperate minutes held a compulsion for him that he couldn't shake off. He felt nothing but pity for the man in the ring. González needed help. Was that why he was staying? Alec asked himself. To lend a hand if something happened? He stole a quick look at Henry, whose face was ashen. It told more plainly than words how he too felt about the drama that was taking place.

Rain splattered from González' hat as he looked down at the sand. There was no point in going on, the big man decided. The bull had learned too fast and too well, and El Dorado was slipping. He glanced past the bull to the red *toril* door, signaling to have it opened.

The herdsman above the door shouted, "Whuh-hey, Toro! Whuh-hey!"

But the bull did not turn toward the herdsman or the open door. His eyes remained on the horse and rider. After a few seconds he charged again.

González scowled with the coming of the bull and touched his horse nervously. He watched the bull turn with El Dorado and lower his head. Bracing himself in his right stirrup, González took aim with his lance and struck hard at the bull, but he jabbed too soon. The blunt end of the pole struck the bull high on the withers and slid off without stopping him. El Dorado reared just in time to avoid the horns that swept beneath his forelegs. Hooking suddenly to the right with his head held high, the bull whipped the pole out of González' hand. It fell to the sand as the horse whirled away and the bull turned, renewing the attack.

As González twisted in his saddle his hat flew off and landed in the wet sand. He rode across the ring as if to use the open door himself, but the bull quickly blocked his way. Breathing hard, González brought El Dorado to a stop, his eyes upon the bull — and they were suddenly filled with fear.

Whatever emotion or impulse had driven the big man to fight brave bulls had run dry, and his fear was quickly transferred to his mount. Where only minutes before strength had flowed between horse and rider nothing was left now but sheer terror. Both sought escape from the ring and the bull.

González rode cautiously along the *barrera* trying to go around the bull. His seat and hands were those of a careless rider wanting to bend close to the neck of his horse and *run away*.

Across the ring the black bull bided his time as if he knew he was in complete control. His eyes were afire, brightening more and more as the annoying calls of the herdsman above the open door rang in his small ears. Finally he lowered his wide horns and charged the horse.

An icy terror froze Alec as he watched the bull sweep through pools of rain water. Thunder rolled from the clouds, drowning out the beat of his hoofs. It was the forked lightning streaking the sky that shattered Alec's immobility. The boy's hands moved across the top of the *barrera*. He saw González make a desperate effort to avoid the circle of horns and El Dorado rearing and coming down close to the *barrera*. The bull slipped in his eagerness to reach the horse and fell to both knees. El Dorado stumbled against him and almost went down. The force of the impact sent González forward in his saddle; frantically the man sought something to hold on to but found himself clutching at the air. As Alec pulled himself over the *barrera*, González was thrown upon the black haunches of the bull and then slid to the ring.

While Henry screamed at him, Alec took several running strides across the wet arena. He picked up the large round hat and thrust it in the bull's face, shouting at González to jump the fence.

As the bull struggled to his feet in the mud and slime, he butted the leather hat, almost tearing it from Alec's grasp. By this time El Dorado had already swept through the open *toril* door and González was waiting for Alec before climbing the *barrera*.

Just then the sharp horns pierced the hat and tossed it up in the air. It landed between the bull's black forehoofs. Luckily the bull went for the hat again rather than for the boy. While Alec rushed to the fence the bull lowered his head and slashed at the hat until it lay in shreds.

Later Alec and Henry stood quietly in González' bedroom, waiting for the big man to speak. María, who was also present, didn't need to be told what had happened in the ring. She had only to look at the man's eyes. They were hurt and ashamed.

"You cheated Death today," she said. "You may not be so lucky again. There will not always be someone in the *barrera* brave enough to rescue you."

Irritated, González said sharply, "Go about your work, María. I do nothing that is not of my own choosing."

The woman did not leave. From outside

came the barking of dogs in the silence of early evening. In the distance could be heard the tinkle of cattle bells and the occasional bellow of a big bull.

Alec turned from the open window to the man. He lay there in bed, listless and worn out and uninterested in everything, his eyes dull and staring at the ceiling. Except for the shaking up he had suffered when the bull heaved up beneath him, he had not been hurt.

What if those curved horns had found their mark? Alec wondered. He would never forget the fiery eyes and the flared nostrils as the bull had gone for the lure instead of González or himself. But even more vividly he recalled the previous night when death had seemed imminent time and time again. He wanted no more of the black bulls.

Henry had gone over to the bed. "You owe Alec a lot," he said quietly to Angel González.

"I know that."

"Enough to tell him who sired those colts? It wasn't El Dorado."

"No, it wasn't."

Alec moved over to the bed, as surprised as Henry by the man's ready confession. He waited for González to go on.

"Then what stallion was it?" Henry persisted.

"I'll take you there. I was told to expect you . . . although not quite as soon as this."

"By whom?"

"You'll find out soon enough. It is only a few hours' flight."

"To where?"

"That too you shall learn presently." González turned to the woman. "María, call Luis. Tell him we fly to the Pass tonight." His dark gaze returned to Henry. "That is, unless you'd rather not go?"

"We'll go," Henry answered without consulting Alec. "Don't worry about that none."

"I'm not worrying," the big man said. "I'm not worrying at all. I've been there many times."

8 BLACK WINGS

The giant aircraft wailed in the night, its four engines straining against a strong headwind. Except for a few small lights the cabin was dark. Alec stood beside the Black's stall, his hand on the stallion, while Henry sat in a nearby bucket seat.

"He's getting to be a flying horse," Alec said, trying to sound casual.

The trainer's face was pressed close to a window despite the pitch-blackness of the night. A fork of lightning shattered the darkness and Henry groaned. "Lucky for us we didn't leave him behind," he said. "This is no short trip of a few hours like González said."

"How long's it been?" Alec asked.

"I don't know. My watch has stopped. But it should be daylight before long."

A roll of thunder rocked the aircraft and then a heavy sheet of rain began to beat against the window. "It's not so pretty out there," Henry commented.

Alec rubbed the Black's neck. The stallion was quiet. There was nothing to worry about. Not yet, at any rate. "Have you been able to make out what we're flying over?" he asked.

"Not now. There was water for a while, plenty of it. Maybe we're crossing the Atlantic again," Henry suggested with feigned lightness.

"More likely the Mediterranean Sea," Alec said, going to the window. He waited for the lightning to strike again and when it did he thought he could make out mountains below. Down there big and little things seemed to merge, but at least he knew they were no longer over water. Turning to Henry, he said, "I wouldn't be surprised if we were over Italy and going on."

"Have it *your* way then," the trainer retorted, still attempting light humor. "It's as good a direction as mine."

They closed their eyes, hoping the time would pass more quickly, and finally they dozed fitfully. When they awakened the rain had stopped and the plane was descending. Towering, jagged mountain peaks rose outside the windows, and suddenly they felt more alone than ever. They shivered as with cold and the aircraft went through a heavy layer of rolling clouds.

A few minutes later the night was clear again and they looked below for the flickering lights of a city or village or house. They saw only the jagged mountains surrounding them on all sides. The Black snorted and thunder rolled again. As the plane flew lower its engines whined louder than ever.

Henry said, "They're buzzing somebody down there." He peered into the swelling blackness. "Where do you think we are anyway? Not that it matters."

"Maybe the Balkans."

"Why there?"

Alec didn't answer.

There was a sickening drop to the aircraft, then a distinct braking of the wing flaps as they went into a steep glide. The plane was landing somewhere. Alec reached for the Black's halter.

Now the jagged rock and pointed crags were very close. The plane shot past a gleaming waterfall and went on, dropping lower and lower until a narrow pass or rift between two lofty mountains could be seen.

"The Pass," Alec said as the plane swept through it.

"I guess this is it then," Henry agreed.

There was a slight screech of rubber tires finding hard ground. The aircraft rolled almost to a stop, turned, and taxied for another mile before the engines were shut off. Then there was complete silence.

Alec and Henry put their faces to the window but could see only looming shadows. Angel González joined them without a word. His heavy figure was stooped and he looked suddenly like an old man.

Henry looked at him strangely and asked, "We're to get off here?"

The big man nodded, hunching his shoulders still more as he thrust his hands into his pockets. Going to the door, he opened it, and with Henry's help lowered the mobile ramp from inside the plane.

Tired of his confinement, the Black left the plane eagerly, his head held high and nostrils quivering. He listened to the long wail of a distant animal. There were no stars to be seen overhead, no moon, nothing but shadowy peaks and rocks and crags. The green and red lights of the plane blinked on and off.

Henry said angrily, "What's this anyway,

González? There's nobody here! Nothing at all!"

"It is simply a question of waiting now."

"For whom?" Henry asked.

"You will see," came the nervous reply. "They will meet you."

Alec let the Black graze, concentrating on him so as to be able to stand the terrifying stillness that had enveloped them all. He listened to the quick, keen cut of his horse's teeth as the stallion moved even farther away from the plane in search of better grass. Henry joined them.

Suddenly the Black raised his head and whistled an alarm. Far beyond the black wastes Alec saw a flickering light along the horizon. Was it the first beginnings of dawn? Long minutes passed but the light grew no brighter. He felt terribly cold and reached for his horse. The Black was shaking, either in eagerness to fight or with fear.

"Henry," Alec said, "are you watching that light?"

"Yes," the man replied slowly. "The false dawn, that's all it is. Don't let it bother you."

From behind them came the loud eruption of the aircraft's engines. They jumped for the plane together, their hands pounding its side. The rushing slipstream from the engines almost spun them around and they pressed their bodies into it. The aircraft moved away, its lights blinking.

"*González!*" Henry screamed at the top of his lungs. "*González!*"

He and Alec ran after the plane, shouting into the wind, "*Why, González, why? Don't leave us alone here! What are you doing, González? What are you doing? Wait for us! Come back, González! Come back! You can't leave us here!*"

Nothing but the mounting roar of the plane answered their questions. Faster and faster it went, drawing farther and farther away until it became airborne.

In numbed silence Alec and Henry watched the plane's lights disappear in the clouds. A strong wind came up and swept across the land. It moved the grass at their feet and changed the shapes in the night. It struck them in the face and they hunched forward to meet it. It bit at Alec's hand and flapped the leather lead shank he was holding. He said, almost too quietly to be heard, "Henry, why did he do it to us? What kind of a game is he playing?"

"I don't know."

"He said someone would meet us."

"I heard that too."

"You think he was lying?"

"We'll soon find out," Henry answered gravely.

The wind marked the swift approach of dawn, and soon a distinct line of light appeared on the horizon. At first it was only a faint, luminous glow but then it began climbing ever higher in the sky. The masses of rock round about changed from black to gray.

Henry and Alec watched the east anxiously. The sun should be up soon. Even before they saw it climb over the horizon the tops of the mountains were ablaze with its rays. Then it came forth, a red, glowing ball.

They waited in silence, watching the land about them take shape in detail. They were in a long, narrow valley with a pass at one end through which the plane had come and gone. On every other side rose steep hills of rock and dirt, split by pointed crags and deep rifts. High above them towered lofty peaks, some snow-covered.

Alec and Henry kept moving in an attempt to warm their chilled bodies. The Black snorted at the song of a lone bird, then lowered his head to graze again. Alec's eyes were drawn by what seemed to be a black-rimmed plateau high up on the northern slope of the mountains. All the crags and winding canyons in the area seemed to run up to that great tableland.

Henry said, "Maybe our wait is going to be longer than we think. González left us some food." The trainer had picked up a saddlebag from the ground. In it were dried meat and beans. "Want some?"

The boy shook his head. "Not yet. Do you really think anyone will meet us, Henry?"

"Sure. Don't you?"

"I don't know," Alec answered. The sun was inching skyward with agonizing slowness and the wind blew stronger. The sound of it in this high and lonely place bothered him more than the flying dust and dirt that peppered his face. He talked to the Black, seeking solace in his horse.

They waited in strained silence, but as the sun rose so did their spirits. The wind, too, quit blowing so hard. Yet as more time passed and still no one came to meet them, they began to feel imprisoned and trapped. They exchanged steady looks, each seeking to read a means of escape in the other's eyes.

"It's early yet," Alec said.

"It's been a long time," Henry countered. "We'd better go. We can try to find somebody or at least a sign of somebody havin' been here before . . . maybe tracks even."

"Which way?" Alec asked.

"Whichever way he'll take us." Henry

gestured in the Black's direction. "This is wild country, but we have a horse who knows the wild. We'll let him show us the way. If there are other horses around he'll find them."

They turned to watch the tall stallion and listened to the familiar sound of his teeth tearing the grass. At that moment nothing interested the Black so much as his own hunger. Soon, though, he would scent the wind. Stretched before him was a maze of gorges, ravines, canyons and washes. Which path would he choose and where would it lead them?

9 BLACK WIND

The Black raised his head, suddenly restless and alert. The wind blew in gusts, and despite the climbing sun the morning continued to be icy cold. Alec went to his horse, cupping the Black's muzzle in both hands for warmth and comfort.

Henry said, "Send him on his way. See if he doesn't lead us to some tracks."

Alec set the stallion's head into the mountain wind. "Let's go, black horse," he said, watching the ears.

As he walked beside the Black, his confidence returned. It might take a little time, he told himself, but they'd find their way to safety.

Only when he lifted his gaze to the unreal shape of the peaks looming above did he have any doubts. He frowned as his eyes squinted into the blaze of the morning sun and suddenly he felt terribly *alone* beneath the vastness of the mountains and sky. His hand tightened on the Black's leather lead shank.

The stallion turned to the north of the sun, and soon he began snorting and neighing, talking the language of the wild. *A few moments later they came to a road leading from the valley.*

"What'd I tell you!" Henry said, running forward.

The fine dirt and dust were marked with the hoofprints of many horses. Henry studied the edges of the prints and said, "They're pretty old."

"Perhaps made by the Sales yearlings?" Alec asked.

"Could be," Henry answered. "They're light enough."

Alec pointed down the road. "Look, Henry, wheel marks!"

They studied the deep marks in the soft ground. "A carriage or a wagon," Henry said, "and a heavy one. The hoofprints here are different, too. These were made by heavier horses and more recently."

They followed the winding tracks up the side of a mountain, stopping often to reexamine the ground. It was deathly quiet except for the pull of the Black's hoofs in the earth. The sun climbed higher and reddened their faces. By midmorning they came to a small plateau where a rushing stream broke the stillness. Here the Black paused, drinking for a long while and without hurry. And here, too, in the soft banks of the stream, were the marks of many hoofprints.

"Let's eat something," Henry said, opening the saddlebag which hung loosely across the stallion's back.

Grasshoppers jumped from beneath the Black's hoofs. A bird circled lazily above them, and in the distance they heard the loud wail of an animal. A bit of dried meat and beans . . . How long was this food supposed to last them? Alec wondered, chewing thoughtfully.

"Might as well get going," Henry said impatiently when they had finished.

The Black paced into the high, bright sun, glad to be on his way again. The narrow road went winding and twisting upward, often offering no protection at all from the sheer precipices that dropped thousands of feet on either side. And always above them rose the bare peaks, so lonely, awesome, and terrible. Without the sun Alec and Henry would have lost all sense of direction, for sometimes they faced south, then north and east and west with the twisting of the road.

"It's not what you'd call a bridle path," Henry grunted.

The road had become more shale than dirt, and only occasionally would they find a track. But they didn't need prints as evidence of the road's use. They had only to look at the banks on the sides, which had been put there to prevent washes during heavy rains. Someone was very much interested in keeping this road open.

The sun grew brighter and hotter and the sweat was caked on the Black's side. Bright-brown water laced the road ruts but none of the travelers stopped to drink it.

Henry said, "This hard going will stiffen him up."

"To say nothing of what it's going to do to us," Alec answered, trying to laugh despite his weariness.

"Why don't you ride? Your weight won't bother him much."

Alec shook his head. "When you walk, I walk. It would be different if we could take turns riding him."

Henry snorted. "I wouldn't put a leg up on him for all the mountain climbs in the world!

How long do you think I'd last? He won't tolerate me the way he does you, you know."

Alec didn't answer.

"It can't be much farther," Henry said, slipping on a loose stone.

Another hour passed and their doubts and fears grew stronger as the sky clouded and the land became more desolate. The wind, too, came up again, twisting its way through the jagged rock to meet them. It was icy cold. They no longer talked to each other but bent into the gale and listened, keeping their mouths tightly closed because of the flying grit. In the great distances they thought they heard the scream of a stallion . . . or was it the wind? The Black did not answer it but continued on his way with no change in pace or gait. Only once did he dance sideways and that was because he smelled a fast-flowing stream.

They stopped then, but when they went on again there seemed to be no escape from the sharp grains of gravel and dirt which tore at their faces. They became more and more desperate in seeking relief. Their eyes burned and their lips were cracked and swollen and cold. Sometime later they reached another plateau where the ground was soft and pock-marked with the prints of many horses. But their only interest was that here the wind swept over grass rather than shale and dirt.

They made a rough camp under some high rocks that jutted out from the western wall. There was no escaping the icy blasts but the wind was clear and free of grit. Alec tethered the Black and with Henry gathered all the wood they could find and started a fire. Warming themselves, too cold and tired to talk, they stood beside the wind-driven flames in sober silence. Not until the fire scorched their faces and clothes did they move away, and then only a step.

Alec said, "When the wind dies down we'll go on."

Henry didn't answer. His face was grim and gray beneath the grizzled stubble of his beard. He looked past the fire to the great tableland above them, guessing that it must be there that their journey would end. *If the wind would only stop. . . . Why must they endure this? What had they done to González to be left alone? Why? Why?*

Coming down from the great heights, the wind grew in intensity with the passing of the long afternoon hours, giving them no respite, no chance to go on, shattering the gloom of the fast approaching night.

From the saddlebag Alec took the dried meat

and gave half of it to Henry. They warmed it on the ends of long sticks, jealously guarding it from the golden flames. When they had finished, Henry said, "If I should fall asleep standing up, pull me out of the fire."

Alec watched the Black and the whirling sky. It seemed the whole world was speeding by and he felt tiny beneath the immensity of it all. . . . Where were they and where would this end? Would they find anyone at all? He listened to the wind mingled with the swift rush of a nearby stream.

Then Alec went to his horse and staked him closer to the fire. The Black bumped his head against him and Alec put a hand around the horse's neck, finding comfort and warmth in his nearness. Henry still stood by the fire, his eyes closed. An owl hooted in the distance, its call wavering with the wind. Henry opened his eyes, looked around, and then without a word sat down, resting his head on upraised knees. Alec rebuilt the fire and sat down beside his friend. He, too, closed his eyes but his ears were alert to every sound.

Beyond the dim canyons and ravines came the howling of wolves. Occasionally Alec opened his eyes to check the fire and look at the snow-capped mountaintops that rimmed the plateau. Tomorrow they would reach the great tableland which rested at the foot of the highest peak of all. He shivered with cold despite the fire. He had no doubt that before long the ground would be white and shimmering with frost. He pulled his light sweater about him, rubbing his arms and moving as close as possible to the fire. If they kept the fire going, they'd be all right. He hated to think what it would be like without it. He closed his eyes again, and even though the heat scorched his eyebrows it felt very good.

The empty saddlebag lay beside Alec. The Black moved into the circle of firelight, pulling mouthfuls of dry brittle grass from the ground with each step. The wind swept across the silence of the night, ruffling the horse's mane and tail; it bent the flames and sent sparks flying into the cold night.

Alec had no intention of going to sleep but his weariness was deep and overwhelming. It left no room for concern or thoughtfulness, only dreams.

He dreamed of home and his mares and colts and barns. He smelled the scents he loved, the well-oiled leather and saddle soap, the hay and grain. He heard the broodmares rustling their straw bedding and the soft nickering of foals. For him there was no place in the world like Hopeful Farm.

When Alec awakened the fire was almost out

and the ground was white with frost. It was very calm and cold with no rolling clouds to blanket the moon and star-studded sky. He turned quickly to his horse, standing very still and black on the white ground. Then he rose and went to him, even though he knew that his first duty was to rebuild the fire.

Alec did not touch the Black but stood beside him and listened. The rush of the stream was strangely loud in the silence. From far off a boom of thunder rolled, or it might have been a rock slide. There was a rasp of wings high in the air. From beyond the dim ravines came the howl of wolves. It was none of these sounds that had awakened him, that had sent him so quickly to his horse. He stared into the night, shaking as he stared. Nothing stirred, not even the smoke of the dying fire.

From the night came the long agonized wailing of an animal, one terribly hurt or afraid. It continued for a long while but neither Alec nor the Black moved. Their eyes searched the night together.

Alec felt the gaze of someone, something, upon them. He sought to keep his head, telling himself that it was only the night and the cold and the strange mountains that made him feel as he did. But he had only to look at the Black to know how wrong he was. His horse, too, was frightened. Despite the cold, beads of perspiration appeared on Alec's brow. A nameless terror grew within him as he became more and more certain that hidden eyes were prying upon him and his horse.

"Hello!" he shouted into the night. "Hello! Will you help us? Hello!"

A gust of wind raced across the land and it was strangely warm. It kindled the fire, sending a single glowing flame into the darkness, and then whipped away, leaving the night deathly still again. Henry slept undisturbed by Alec's calls. The boy thought he saw a streak of red light stab the depths of the canyons. He couldn't be sure but it was enough to cause a chill to creep over him; with it came a terrible loneliness. He touched his horse.

The stallion did not turn to Alec; he shivered with cold or fright. A lone, heavy cloud passed across the moon and the night became pitch-dark.

Suddenly the Black's nostrils flared and he turned his head. Alec turned with him, instantly alert, for he knew that his horse had picked up a scent. This was something he could understand, and he shook off the strange, uncanny chill with which he had been seized. The Black, too, was no longer trembling. Eagerly he searched the darkness, and then, without further warning, he screamed his ringing blast of hate and defiance. He pricked up his ears and whistled again. From the Black this meant only one thing: He had scented another stallion.

The moon moved from behind the cloud and its light bathed the frosty plateau. Alec saw a distant light that made him afraid to shout or move. It was similar to the red light he'd seen in the depths of the canyons and now it was above him! At first it appeared only as a small spot glowing in the night. But at the Black's repeated whistles it appeared to drop into the sheer abyss that separated the plateau from the adjoining mountain. It moved slowly in a side-long way almost as if it were flying. It descended for several hundred feet and then vanished altogether.

Alec closed his eyes and shook his head before reopening them. The moon was playing tricks with him . . . the moon and the night shadows and this lonely land. The Black whistled again, reared, and bolted. If Alec had not been holding tightly on to the lead shank he would have gotten away.

The stallion's whistle and actions proved there had to be a horse up there, regardless of how impossible it seemed.

Henry suddenly appeared at Alec's side. "What is it?" he asked. "What's he screaming about?"

His question didn't require any answer for

there, in the moonlight, silhouetted against the bare rock of the nearby mountains, was a running horse!

The Black plunged forward but with Henry's help Alec was able to hold him. Their hearts turned cold when they saw the trail of phosphorescent sparks the horse was streaming in his wake! It was a shimmering streak of blue and red and orange lights. It swept from the mountainside into the depths and then was gone. But coming closer was the beat of a horse's hoofs! Louder and louder and louder they became until Alec and Henry clamped their hands over their ears to shut out the sound. The Black reared and plunged and snorted but there was nothing for him to fight except the beat of hoofs resounding from the mountain walls. Finally they quieted and all that could be heard was the return of the searing, icy wind.

What riderless horse had Alec and Henry seen in the ghostly aura of the mountains? Where had he gone? And was it his dismal neighing that had awakened Alec?

10 BLACK MAGIC

Alec and Henry watched for the horse to reappear, their eyes watering from the constant strain of peering into the distance. But they saw nothing, no weird trail of blue and orange lights, no natural sparks of horseshoes striking flint. The Black moved and the sound of his hoofs crackled in their ears.

"Easy," Alec whispered to him. "It's all right."

Yet the boy continued searching the night while he held his horse. What sort of place had they come to? What horse could run where there was no trail, streaming flaming sparks behind him? Who used this road and where did it lead? Shivering in every limb, Alec went over to the fire. It had almost died down and Henry was seated beside it with his head in his hands, staring at the dull embers.

Alec added wood to the fire. "Did we really see him?" he asked.

"The horse?"

"Was it a horse?"

"Of course it was," Henry snapped. "I know a horse when I see one. Better than a man sometimes."

"Even a ghost horse?"

"A horse is a horse." Henry's face was flushed, his eyes bright.

"On such a night in such a place it's easy to be fooled. We couldn't have seen those sparks."

Henry didn't answer.

Dawn was coming and the jagged terrain took on a ghostlike appearance. Early mists danced in the light of the setting moon. Alec walked around the fire to relieve the stiffness of his legs and back.

Henry said, "Once there was a horse named Firetail. He got his name because he raced as though his tail was on fire. He did a mile in one minute and four seconds."

"That's ridiculous," Alec said. "No horse could run that fast. The world record is one minute thirty-three and a fraction."

"I know," Henry said quietly. "But no horse ever ran with his tail on fire either."

"When did this Firetail race?" Alec asked.

"Around 1770."

"Then his time is as legendary as he is."

"Maybe the time's legendary but not him," Henry said. "He was a real honest-to-goodness horse."

Alec forced himself to laugh. "Are you suggesting we saw his ghost tonight?"

"No, but we saw a tail on fire sure enough. It wasn't the night or the place that fooled us."

The first gray light brightened the high peaks. It descended slowly until it finally found the blackness of the bottom land and turned it to a leaden color. Then the road took shape and Henry and Alec decided it was safe to go on.

Alec, leading the Black, followed Henry across the frosted grass. He was glad to be on the move for his legs were stiff and his fingers numb. He rubbed them hard, not so much for warmth as to make certain he was really awake and walking into another day. The night before might well have been a horrible nightmare. The improved circulation in his hands, providing him with warmth if not comfort, convinced him he wasn't being deceived.

The road rose above them, and with daybreak came distant animal howls and wailing. Alec didn't recognize the cry.

Henry said, "Here are more wheel tracks so it shouldn't be too bad for us on foot."

"I'd rather walk this road than drive it," Alec answered, looking over the side embankment into vast, black depths.

They were within the shadows of the great tableland. Above it towered a sheer wall of rock, rising for what seemed thousands of feet before its smoothness was shattered by cliffs and crags mounting to a snow-capped peak. As they gazed skyward they knew their eyes had played tricks on them the night before. No horse in the world could have traveled up there.

The road to the tableland was not so steep as it appeared from below, and they found themselves looking into deep rifts and canyons. They saw patches of sea-green forests and gorges white with water. Most of the time, however, they kept their eyes on the road.

They neared the overhanging lip of the tableland, their spirits rising with the end of the climb. Even the Black snorted as if with joy. A faint breeze stirred, coming from the land above. It was clean and pungent with pine and cedar. They traveled faster and faster, eager to see what lay ahead.

"After all," Henry said, "it wouldn't have

taken us so long if it hadn't been for that wind and we'd kept goin'."

When they reached the tableland they stopped in awe, realizing they had not prepared themselves for its beauty and magnificence. Nor had they, by any figment of the imagination, expected to find a large fountain playing water upon a marble statue of a boy and a rearing horse!

They said nothing while their astounded gazes left the fountain for the land beyond. It was deeply rolling and not as large an area as they had expected. It went back into the mountain in the shape of a horseshoe and was bordered on two sides by a thick forest of pine and cedars. It was protected against the biting winds of the upper air, yet so situated as to receive the full benefits of the sun. Meandering mountain streams watered the lush green grass and the air was warm without being hot.

"Well, what d'ya know!" Henry gasped. "It's like a fairy tale on top of a nightmare!"

They turned again to the spraying fountain. The boy could have been Alec, the horse the Black. They looked at it for many minutes and then their astonished gazes searched for the people who must live here.

They followed the road as it ran close to the forest. Farther ahead a high stone wall with a great gate in the center crossed the tableland. They knew their destination was on the other side of the wall and hurried faster than ever, crossing a wooden bridge that had been built over a hand-dug ravine, some thirty feet wide and twenty deep. There was a small stream running through it and they had no doubt that at one time it had been used as a moat to keep invaders from the wall beyond.

They were hardly prepared for the sudden opening of the big gate, much less the appearance of a horse-drawn carriage! They fell back, taking hold of each other's arm, their eyes unbelieving.

The Black nickered, for the horses were mares and he looked upon their approach with as much interest as Alec and Henry did. There were two pairs — four chalk-white Arabians — and they came through the gate in a long striding walk, their tails and manes crimped and flowing. Their hindquarters moved in a slightly swinging motion and their small heads were bent gracefully, nodding up and down almost as if to attract the Black's attention.

Alec and Henry knew they were looking at Arabians of the purest strain. They were small horses even though their perfect conformation made them appear larger. Their ears were small and delicately pointed, set wide apart as were the eyes. Their necks were slender and long, flowing nobly into short, wide backs from which floated luxurious tails. Even at a walk they seemed to soar, their hoofs barely touching the ground before coming up again.

Henry muttered, "We'ye found them, Alec."

The boy didn't answer, for the horses had broken into a trot and he was absorbed in watching the clean, fluid line of their strides as they approached. Only when he was convinced that Henry was right did his eyes leave the horses for the carriage.

The driver sat on a high seat, holding reins and whip expertly, and wearing black-and-gold livery. The carriage, all black except for the golden paneled doors, was an open one and the back seats were occupied by two men and a woman. When it came to a stop a soft voice said, "Welcome home, Shêtân. We've been waiting for you."

11 BLACK WELCOME

Shêtân was the Black's Arabic name and few people knew it.

It was the woman who had spoken, and she watched the tall stallion snatch playfully at the neck of the nearest mare. Alec recognized her but she looked far different from the person he remembered. Was that so strange, though? He had last seen her as a growing girl. Now she was a woman.

Tabari, the daughter of Abu Ishak, who had bred the Black!

She had been a young rider whose reckless desert spirit had roused the pride of every Bedouin. Now she sat with a prim and formal attitude in the deep leather cushions of her luxurious carriage. Yet she seemed friendly and sincere as she added, "And you, too, Alec and Henry, welcome!"

Alec said bewilderedly, "Tabari, I can't believe it!"

She smiled without a word, and at close range Alec realized again how much of the girlishness he'd known had vanished. He found her every look guarded, if not unfriendly. So he waited for her to speak, sensing that it would be better to let her lead the conversation.

The man beside her said graciously, "I, too, bid you welcome." His voice was loud yet casual, his eyes bright and direct.

Tabari's husband, Sheikh Abd-al-Rahman, had changed far less than she, but that was only natural, for he had already reached maturity when they had last seen him in Arabia. Now his short black beard was thrust into his chest as he extended a hand to them in greeting.

Alec shook the hand that was offered to him, then turned back to Tabari, who was smiling as if to herself. "Is he not everything we'd heard?" she asked her husband quietly.

Abd-al-Rahman's eyes lighted. "Of course," he replied, reaching out from the carriage to place a lean brown hand upon the stallion's back. The man whistled softly. "He's all you said, Tabari."

"Naturally," she replied sweetly.

Henry spoke for the first time. "You sound like you expected us," he said as politely as he could.

"We did," the Sheikh answered, "but not so soon. Unfortunately we did not hear the plane nor Angel's signal. But then it was such a bad night."

Tabari laughed gaily at their immediate surprise, and her raven-black hair rippled about her neck as she tossed her head back. "You look so frightened, both of you," she said, her eyes flashing.

"But—" Alec began and then stopped, for Abd-al-Rahman had joined his wife in laughter. Their voices rang clearly and sharply in the fragrant air.

Alec stared at Tabari, attracted not by her laughter or what she'd said, but by the sudden recklessness in her eyes. It was as if she'd momentarily thrown off her cloak of maturity and was about to ask if she could ride the Black!

Then Tabari stood up in the carriage, her figure slim and supple in gray gabardine and a yellow scarf knotted around her neck. "Nazar," she said, turning to the third occupant of the carriage, "do not your ancient eyes burn with envy at sight of such a horse? Is he not everything my father dreamed he'd be as a mature stallion?" Her eyes remained on the old man who sat quietly opposite her and her husband.

Obediently Nazar turned and looked at the horse, but his stare was vacant and disinterested. Of the three he was the only one wearing complete Arab dress. A red shawl that matched the flowing garment he wore over his slight body covered his head. When he finally turned his wrinkled face toward Tabari his expression had changed, his eyes becoming very alert and keen. But he said nothing.

"He is very old and tired," Tabari told the others softly. "He can neither speak nor hear but he reads my lips easily. He was my father's dearest and most devoted servant. Now he wills that I return him to our native land to meet Allah."

She spoke reverently of Allah yet her accent was very British as were her clothes, her Victorian carriage, and her liveried coachman. While her husband's accent was British as well, his appearance was more striking, a mixture of the East and the West. His dark face was framed by a flowing white head shawl secured by a cord as jet-black as his beard. His six-foot lean figure, however, was clothed in whipcord breeches, gleaming English riding boots, and a dark blue sweater.

Tabari sat down again, and for a fleeting second Alec thought he saw a shadow of deep sorrow flit across her face. Then it was gone and a slow smile crept about her mouth.

"You must return home with our distinguished guests," she said sweetly to Abd-al-Rahman, "and see that they are comfortable. It is not often that we are so honored."

The Black was attempting to bite the mares again, and Alec pulled him away without taking his eyes off Tabari and her husband. He listened to them talk as if this were some casual meeting in a park at home.

Abd-al-Rahman smiled patiently at his wife. He looked like a good-humored hawk as he leaned over and patted her hand. "You know the road is dangerous by carriage," he said. "I like to be with you."

In sudden anger Tabari withdrew her hand and said, "Your sitting next to me doesn't help and Jason knows every foot of the way. It will not be the first time I have traveled it alone." She sat back, her features set and proud.

The Sheikh continued smiling. "It's only that I like to hold your hand along the way." And he swiftly caught her wrist and held it.

For a moment they appraised each other in strained silence. Then Tabari smiled archly.

"I was only thinking of our guests," she said coquettishly.

The Sheikh seemed to be turning over in his mind what his wife had said but he did not speak or look away.

"And it is strange, is it not," she went on, laughing, "that you let me fly alone but do not trust me on our very own road?"

Abd-al-Rahman listened as though fascinated. When finally he spoke, however, it was in short sentences. "Go then." A flush came over his face. "Be careful. Perhaps I never should have taught you to fly."

Her eyes opened wide. "But it was you who suggested it!"

"So I did," he said glumly. "So I did." Then, kissing her lightly on the mouth, he stepped out of the carriage. "All right, Jason," he said to the driver. "Guide your horses well."

"Yes, sir."

Tabari, glancing at Alec and Henry, said, "See that he makes you comfortable, my friends." Her gaze swept to the Black. "As for Shêtân, his stall has been ready a long, long time."

Astonished by Tabari's parting remark Alec watched the carriage speed across the bridge. What had she meant? He turned to Abd-al-Rahman. "Are we in Arabia?" he asked. "Is that what Tabari meant by saying the Black's stall was ready for him?"

The young Sheikh's eyes followed the fast-moving carriage as he answered, "No, Alec, we're far from there. This is a stronghold built by Tabari's ancestors centuries before the Black was ever foaled. He has never been here."

Henry spoke. "Just where are we then?"

"That I cannot tell you, old fellow," the Sheikh answered. "I have many enemies who would rob me of my horses if they knew."

Henry snorted. "A good chance they'd have of finding their way here," he said.

By this time the carriage had disappeared in the distance. "You are right of course," Abd-al-Rahman said kindly, "but only because it has been kept secret for a very long time. It was here that the strongest desert chieftains carried on their most important horse-breeding operations. The grass and water are the best, as you can see. It is also well protected against the winds —" he hesitated, smiled and went on — "and raiding parties. There is nothing to fear here from our enemies yet it is central enough to conduct business."

"You must have good horses to make all this worth while," Henry said.

The Sheikh's smile faded. "You should take that for granted, Henry."

"I do," the trainer answered.

"I know. That's why you came."

"Tell me," Alec asked quietly, "how do you know so much? What made you expect us?"

"It's our business to know anything that has to do with fine horses," Abd-al-Rahman answered with a half-smile. His sharp gaze shifted to the Black. "He's as proud as a peacock, isn't he?"

Expecting no reply and getting none, the Sheikh started down the road. "Come, please," he said pleasantly. "It is but a short walk." His body was lean, tall and straight. His strides were those of a desert hunter, springy and quick.

They passed through the carved wooden gate, which opened and closed easily on well-oiled hinges, and found themselves on a widespread and gently rolling plain. The grass here, watered by underground springs, was even more lush than outside the wall. Towering shade trees and foliage were thick; the whole place had an air of summer drowsiness, and the great mountain which served as a backdrop added to the serenity of the scene.

Abd-al-Rahman, glancing back at the gate as if listening for the sound of the carriage, smiled and said, "My wife is like all women. She seeks to love and dominate at the same time. I suppose I have spoiled her, though. There is so little she can do here."

"Doesn't she like it?" Alec asked.

"She prefers home, Alec, or at least vacations in England where we have many old school friends. This is too isolated for any woman and most men. It is why I insisted upon her learning to fly years ago. Now she escapes like a winged bird and returns as willingly."

The road had become a well-attended driveway with white stone fences on the sides separating the plain into field after field. A small band of mares grazed in one pasture and as they approached Alec took firm hold of the Black's lead shank.

Henry said quietly, "These are the race mares, Alec."

It was as simple as that. From this band had come the Sales yearlings they'd seen in America. Unlike the carriage horses these brood mares were large and tall. They had size without coarseness. The Arabian's refinement in conformation and head was there for the world to see. From this type of mare the Black, too, had come. *Where was the sire?*

12   BLACK GHOST

At a turn in the driveway, they left the fields
behind. Soon they came upon an enormous
stone house, rising story after story against the
base of the mountain, and supported by tall
columns. Yet for all its great size there was a
softness to it because of the many beautiful
gardens which surrounded it. Small fountains
played upon statues of animals and birds, all
made from the same golden-colored stone as
the house. There were terraces of flowers
ablaze with color, and fish ponds and sparkling,
rushing streams. It was an intricate maze of
hanging gardens, reservoirs and stonework.

There were men at work, planting, pruning,

and caring for these gardens. They stopped to look at Alec and Henry as the group went by. They were curious without being excited, as if visitors were to be expected. Tall and muscular, they had sharp, dark features but there was no Arabic blood in them. They wore the leather clothes of people whose home was in the high mountains. Obviously they were natives of this land, whatever it was.

Alec and Henry walked slowly beside the young Sheikh, their eyes bewildered at what they saw, and their senses captured by the enchantment of the gardens. The air was spiced with scents of flowers and blossoms, and there was no need to ask who had planned these grounds. It had to be Tabari, for her feminine touch was evident everywhere.

At a fork in the driveway Abd-al-Rahman led them away from the house.

"Come," the Sheikh said, "as horsemen you must first see my stables and, of course, care for your horse."

Directly ahead a high arch in the shape of a giant horseshoe extended over the road, supported by two statues of rearing horses with water spouting from their mouths. Alec and Henry walked beneath the arch, watching the sunlight sparkle upon the golden-colored horses as the fountains splashed upon them.

A few minutes' walk brought them to a

bridge spanning a large stream, whose rippling-white waters were rushing to reach the lower fields. On the other side of the bridge was a great tent more than a hundred feet long and thirty feet wide. It was open at one end and just within the flaps sat a small group of Arabs around a smoking fire. Alec could smell the coffee that was being made.

It might have been a scene in Arabia, and Alec looked beyond the tent, almost expecting to see a herd of camels lying on the ground, patiently waiting for the caravan to move on. Instead he saw only a small flock of grazing sheep and goats.

Abd-al-Rahman explained without stopping, "We brought the most chosen of our tribe with us, mostly for work in the fields and stables. Tabari has no use for them in the house . . . but then they have no use for houses."

Just ahead, deep within the shadows of the trees, was a quadrangle of stables. On top of the iron-barred gateway was a stable clock, its long gilt hands pointing almost to noon. The buildings, consisting of only one story each, were of the same golden-colored stone and architecture as the house.

The Sheikh stopped in the center of the stableyard and addressed Alec. "I'm assuming you want to care for your horse yourself."

"Yes," Alec said. "Where do you want him?"

"Not here," Abd-al-Rahman answered. "Not near the mares. Come."

He led the way to the other end of the stable-yard and through another gate. They went into the forest again, the pine-needled lane rising with the easy slope of the land as it approached the base of the mountain. Near the stream and directly opposite the massive house was a circular barn. Inside were three huge stalls. On the door of the largest and most luxurious of all was a small gold plaque of a young boy and a rearing horse, with emeralds for the boy's eyes and rubies for the horse's.

"Who are they?" Alec asked, recalling the statue he had seen earlier.

For a moment Abd-al-Rahman didn't answer. He opened the door of the adjacent stall and motioned Alec to take the Black inside. Then he said solemnly, "They are the boy who became one of the greatest tribal leaders of my country, and the horse of his young dreams. His name was Barjas ben Ishak, an ancestor of Tabari. He died in 1689."

"Without ever finding his dream horse?" Henry asked, anxious to keep the Sheikh talking. He followed Alec into the Black's stall. There was hay in the rack and a sack of feed below it.

"Yes," Abd-al-Rahman told Henry. "But he raised many fine horses. The best one of all oc-

122

cupied that particular stall. It is not unusual in my country, you know, to choose one horse to idolize even though we may have hundreds. It was so in the case of Barjas ben Ishak."

Alec listened to the conversation while tending his horse. He thought of the big, empty stall next door, bedded down and waiting, just as this one had been ... for what stallion if not the Black?

Henry was prodding Abd-al-Rahman further. "Then it was Barjas ben Ishak who built this place?"

"Yes. In those days, even more so than now, the strongest tribes were those with the finest horses. Their lives depended upon the speed and stamina of their mounts."

Alec left the Black's stall. The sun was shining upon the gold plaque on the adjacent door and the jeweled eyes seemed to be winking at him realistically. He found it difficult to turn away.

"His were a wandering people," the Sheikh went on, "not only from desire but from necessity as well. They needed fertile pastures and good climate for their stock. And then, too, his greatest fear was that his best horses would be stolen. He watched over them as he never did his family. He knew their genealogy from the days of Mohammed and sometimes even before that."

123

Alec turned from the shining figures of the boy and horse and went to the Black again, making sure he had left nothing undone. The stall was large and the bedding thick. The Black had been watered and was whiffing his feed.

Abd-al-Rahman continued, "It was on one of his long journeys north that he heard of this protected mountain plain. Later he brought his finest mares and stallions and built this stronghold. He was confident that if left in peace he would some day produce the stallion of his boyhood dreams, one whose speed would be that of the desert winds and who would sire equally fast colts."

"But he didn't," Henry interjected, for the Sheikh had turned away and the trainer didn't want the conversation to end. It was just getting interesting.

Abd-al-Rahman was looking into the empty stall. "No," he finally said, "but Tabari's father did, centuries later, and using the same foundation stock. He named the young stallion Ziyadah and this is his stall."

The name was not unfamiliar to Alec and Henry. In Arabic it meant *superb in speed*. And Ziyadah had been the Black's sire.

"You mean *was* his stall, don't you?" Henry corrected. "Ziyadah is dead. It says so in the books."

"No, he is very much alive," the Sheikh answered, his dark eyes sweeping over the mountain ridges. "He runs high and fast, so fast that his tail appears to catch on fire. The natives call him Firetail but we know it is our Ziyadah!"

There was a long moment of silence. Then Henry asked, "Why are you so sure?"

"Because of the yearlings we sent to America. They were *his*. Only Ziyadah could stamp his colts in such a way. Truly you are not surprised! Is that not why you and Alec are here? When you looked upon those colts did you not know they came from the same mold as the Black? We knew you would attempt to find their sire."

"And now that we are here?" Alec questioned.

The tall man smiled for the first time. "Now that you are here, Alec, I hope that you and the Black will help me catch Ziyadah!"

The black stallion pushed his head over the stall door, his nostrils swelling as he looked toward the stables beyond. But it was Henry who snorted.

"One moment you say you know it's Ziyadah because he sired the Sales yearlings and now you're asking our help to catch him! How'd you breed the mares?"

"They were pasture bred."

"If Ziyadah runs in the mountains how'd he

125

reach your fields? Your end wall must be thirty feet high."

"We don't know."

"Has he been back since?"

"No, or we might have caught him. We've been waiting."

The mountain silence was broken by a loud shout, then a man's whistle, followed by the dull rumble of running hoofs. The mares were being brought in from the fields. The Black whinnied.

"Come, you are tired and hungry," Abd-al-Rahman said graciously. "Your horse is safe. He will not be bothered for none of our people are allowed here. It was so willed by Tabari's father upon his death."

Alec looked questioningly at a nearby chair with a blanket across it. Overhead hung a black-and-gold braided halter and lead rope.

Following the boy's gaze, Abd-al-Rahman said, "It is only the chair of old Nazar, the mute whom Tabari is taking home. It was he who took care of this barn and of Ziyadah as a colt. It was he who set him free."

They started down the lane toward the stables.

"Intentionally?" Alec asked.

"No. Nazar was most devoted to Tabari and her father. They were the only ones who could read his face and signs. Despite his age and muteness, Nazar had no equal in the care of horses. That is why Abu Ishak put him in charge of his most prized colt."

"Then how'd he let Ziyadah break away from him?" Henry asked.

"Nazar had lavished much love and attention on the young horse," Abd-al-Rahman answered. "Tabari says that Ziyadah followed him around as would a bodyguard. Often he would race in a circle about Nazar until one would have thought the thunder of his hoofs would have broken the old man's lifelong silence."

"But how'd he get away?" Henry persisted.

"I'm coming to that," the Sheikh said patiently. "It seems that Abu Ishak was worried because Ziyadah had started jumping very high and none of the pasture fences could hold him. He therefore ordered the old man to hobble him for fear the young stallion would rake his belly on the stones and become fatally injured. To Nazar this was like clipping the wings of a hawk, so unknown to Abu Ishak he would set Ziyadah free for a while each night. One night the young stallion did not return to him. He has waited all these years, keeping his stall fresh and his halter ready."

"No one saw Ziyadah leave the fields?" Alec asked incredulously.

Abd-al-Rahman shook his head. "It is said that the night riders heard the thunder of his

127

hoofs and that there was a trail of sparks as of horseshoes striking flint. One rider said he saw Ziyadah going over the end wall but that of course was impossible."

"Unless he had wings," Henry mumbled.

"When did the natives first see him after his escape?" Alec asked thoughtfully.

"Shortly after Abu Ishak's death. It is ironical, is it not, that he did not live to know that Ziyadah was not dead after all? He and Tabari had returned to Arabia certain of the young stallion's death, for the bones of a horse had been found in a deep abyss."

"And the natives call him Firetail?" Alec asked, recalling the fiery horse he and Henry had seen the night before.

"Yes, but he is Ziyadah. Of that I'm sure."

"If he sired those colts, you're right," Alec agreed quietly.

13 BLACK HEAT

Abd-al-Rahman's home was like the kind found in a fairy tale, complete with towers and brilliantly colored windows of tinted glass. The Sheikh and Alec and Henry climbed a double flight of stone stairs, stopping before an arched front door. It was opened by two English footmen in black-and-gold livery and white gloves.

Alec hung back, awed by the splendor within, but Henry followed close at the Sheikh's heels. Opening doors, the footmen walked ahead through richly colored rooms with luxurious divans and walls covered with intricate tapestries of carved designs and figures.

The atmosphere was that of ancient Arabia and it reached out and enveloped Alec. Yet he saw too the changes made by Tabari's youthful hands. From the gilt ceilings hung crystal chandeliers. The furniture was modern, more English than Arabian, and a hidden phonograph played soft string music.

Abd-al-Rahman came to a stop. "You must bathe and eat, then we shall talk more," he said, leaving them.

Later, in their rooms, they were served a sumptuous dinner of excellent roast beef and chicken, together with many vegetables and salad. For dessert they had cheese. They spoke little for they were half-famished.

When Henry had finished he sat back and said, "What do you make of what he told us, Alec?"

Alec glanced out the open window overlooking the gardens and fields. "Why would he be lying?"

Henry's gaze shifted to the nearby servants and he said, "For the same reason he registered El Dorado as sire of the Sales yearlings. What reason would he have for doing that when he says it was Ziyadah?"

Alec shrugged his shoulders. "Ask him. Maybe he'll tell you."

"Maybe he will," Henry agreed. "He's talking more now that the boss is gone."

"Boss?"

"Tabari."

"Oh," said Alec.

Henry glanced behind Alec, suddenly aware of the slight figure that had silently approached the table. "Yes?" Henry asked.

The man touched his forehead and breast before saying, "If you are finished, please follow me." His accent was as Arabic as were his features yet he, too, wore the black-and-gold livery of the English house servants.

Henry turned to Alec. "Shall we go?"

"Do you have any other suggestions?" Alec asked. He wasn't joking. He didn't like the looks of the man who was waiting for them to follow him. His eyes, as yellow as a cat's, smoldered even though he smiled and bowed humbly. His body was small and slight, almost gnomish, and he had long scraggly hair that hung down almost to his shoulders. He looked evil, withdrawn, and ancient. He smiled again, patiently awaiting them.

Henry shrugged his shoulders and stood up. "Are you taking us to the Sheikh?" he asked.

There was a nodding of the head, nothing more.

"All right then," Henry said. "Go ahead, Alec."

The man's straw-thin legs moved silently, swiftly, leading the way. He led them along the echoing length of a gallery and then down a flight of deeply carpeted stairs. They passed the front door with its ponderous bars and bolts and went through another hall into a long, green-paneled library. Finally they came to a stop before a closed door.

The servant knocked lightly and then stepped to one side, motioning them to enter. Henry took hold of the large brass knob and turned it slowly. There was a dim light burning in what seemed to be more a stone cavern than a room. Abd-al-Rahman sat in a straight-backed chair before a huge fireplace. There was no fire burning, however, and the dim light came from a small desk lamp.

The Sheikh rose from his chair and closed the door. "Welcome to my house," he said, smiling. "It is here I would live if it were not for my pretty wife." Even though he spoke lightly he seemed to mean what he said. He had removed his fine British clothes and was wearing those of a desert Bedouin, the tight camel's hair breeches and short jacket bearing the rips and sweat stains of many long and rough rides. For the first time since Alec and Henry had met him he did not have a hat on, and they noticed that his hair, like his beard, was cropped short.

"I do hope Homsi was gracious," Abd-al-Rahman said. "Often he is inclined not to be. It is his defense because of his small size. Tabari objects to him but there is nothing I can do. Or *want* to do," he added, smiling again. "His body is little but his heart is great. We grew up together and he has served and guarded me well. It is customary in my country, as you probably know, to have such a close, personal servant and I am afraid Tabari must put up with him."

Alec and Henry were so occupied in looking about the room that they scarcely took in what their host was saying. There were two long, narrow stained-glass windows flanking the great fireplace. Except for three hard chairs and a desk, there was no furniture. There were a few books and the lamp on the desk. Nothing could be more simple than this room — or was it a cell? Gone was the splendor to be seen on the other side of the door. Gone were the hanging gardens and playing fountains. This was the room of a solitary man.

The heavy layer of dust over everything made Alec aware that despite Abd-al-Rahman's greeting, the Sheikh spent little time here. Whose room had it been?

"This was where Abu Ishak worked out his horse-breeding program," the Sheikh said, a slight uneasiness in his tone. "He did not want it used by anyone else but since I am carrying on his work . . ."

He did not finish but turned to the desk, his fingers nervously tracing the dust.

"Perhaps we can talk somewhere else then," Henry suggested. He could feel his temples throbbing. He blamed it on the heat and dust of the small, closed room. Or was it some undefinable fear? Had Abu Ishak wanted this room kept closed for a special reason? Was that why Abd-al-Rahman too acted so jittery?

"No, it is best that we stay here," the Sheikh told Henry. "You will better understand what I have to say."

Alec asked, "You mean the paper work Abu Ishak did here led to Ziyadah?"

"*And* the Black," Abd-al-Rahman admitted, nodding his dark head. "It was to this room he came when Tabari was a little girl. From Arabia he had brought his finest horses and for the same reason as his great ancestor who had built this stronghold — *because he was fearful of desert raids.* Abu Ishak was confident that he would produce a superior horse if left alone. He carefully fused one strain with another, experimenting as no other sheikh had ever done, even Barjas ben Ishak. Finally he produced Ziyadah and realized his work was almost done."

"*Almost* done," Henry repeated. "I thought you told us Ziyadah had the speed of the desert winds."

"But Abu Ishak insisted that the horse must also prove himself as a sire, one who would pass down his speed and stamina to his colts. He arranged the first and what proved to be the last mating. He sent to Arabia for *Jinah Al-Tayr....*"

Alec repeated the name aloud and Abd-al-Rahman's sharp eyes turned to him. "Of course you would know her name, Alec," he said quietly. "She was the dam of the Black, and this was the mating that produced him."

The Sheikh went to the huge fireplace and stood before the old wire screen which guarded a rusty grate. "Her name in Arabic means *wings of the bird,*" he continued, "but Jinah Al-Tayr had lost her wings. She was so old that Abu Ishak had her brought to the court of Ziyadah by cart, for he knew her ancient legs could not have withstood the rigors of the long journey. It was only a few days after the mating that Ziyadah escaped."

Abd-al-Rahman's gaze swept the bare room. "Abu Ishak remained here until mountaineers found the skeleton of a horse which he pronounced that of Ziyadah. Then he left this room and house never to return."

Henry moved toward the door. "Later in Arabia, Jinah Al-Tayr foaled the Black, is that it?" he asked.

The Sheikh nodded. "Yes, and Abu Ishak watched him grow with great pride, knowing Ziyadah lived again." He paused, smiling. "Please do not leave, Henry," he asked most graciously.

Henry did not like the Sheikh's smile any more than he did the room. "I thought you were done," he said.

Abd-al-Rahman's smile disappeared. "No, as a matter of fact, it is only here that I enter the story. What I have told you I have learned from Tabari."

The Sheikh returned to the desk, his right hand coming down on it with such force that the lamp rocked on its base, throwing its unsteady gleam into the deep shadows of the room.

Alec shifted his feet uneasily upon the stone floor. He felt the heat and closeness of the room more than ever as the Sheikh suddenly turned his dark eyes on him.

"Little did Abu Ishak dream that the final result of all his work and that of his ancestors would be responsible for his own death. If he had not already willed the Black to you, Alec, Tabari would have had him destroyed on the very spot where he threw her father. It is ironical, is it not, that while both Ziyadah and his first son are here Abu Ishak is dead?"

Henry had moved back from the door. "Not only ironical but most interesting," he said. "How do *you* figure in all this?"

"Only through Tabari and my own interest in fine horses," the Sheikh answered soberly. "When reports reached me in the desert of Ziyadah's ghost being seen by the native mountaineers I knew he was not dead after all. I do not believe in ghosts or wizards or magic of any kind."

"You went after him?"

Abd-al-Rahman nodded. "Tabari was in England for a short stay, seeing friends and recovering from the loss of her father. I sent for her and moved some of our people and best mares here. I knew that if I was fortunate enough to recapture Ziyadah I could carry on Abu Ishak's work as I longed to do."

"And just how did you figure on catching this *ghost* horse?" Henry asked suspiciously.

Abd-al-Rahman smiled but his face was very serious, almost grave, when he answered, "By attracting Ziyadah's attention to our mares."

"It worked but you didn't catch him after all," Henry said. "Did you see him when he came after the mares?"

"Not in the fields but later on the mountain-sides. He ran as they said he did, leaving a trail of sparks behind him and moving like the desert wind."

"He never came down again?" Alec asked.

"No. We have been waiting for over two years with a doubled guard."

"Yet you've seen him during that time?"

"Often," Abd-al-Rahman answered Alec. "He runs where no horse has a right to be. But he is no ghost. He is Ziyadah."

"If you're so certain of that," Henry asked quietly, "why did you register his yearlings under a false sire?"

There was no hesitation in Abd-al-Rahman's reply and only surprise on his face when he said, "But I have told you already that I did not see him in the fields! It is the ancient law of our land that no pure-blooded mare is allowed to be bred except in the presence of witnesses. I could not as leader of my tribe attest that his colts were *asil*, of pure blood, even though I knew they were."

"You mean it would have been dishonest?" Henry asked with sarcasm.

The Sheikh did not smile. "I mean that I do not break our ancient laws!" he said coldly.

"Besides," Abd-al-Rahman went on, in a more conciliatory tone, "the Sales yearlings were only the means to an end. It is Ziyadah I want, and now that you are here I can use your help."

Alec met his gaze. "You mean that since your mares have failed, you want to try something else. You want to send a stud to catch a stud."

"Exactly," the Sheikh answered.

"When?"

"The next time he appears. Perhaps even tonight . . . yes, it might well be tonight. He loves to run when there is a full moon."

14 BLACK ART

That evening Alec looked out his bedroom window into the night. Under the brilliance of a full moon the pasture grass held a tinge of green-gray. It was a peaceful mountain scene. but it offered him little comfort. He hadn't forgotten the new and dangerous note in Abd-al-Rahman's voice when the Sheikh had suggested sending the Black after Ziyadah, perhaps that very night.

Alec had no doubt that his horse could run down Ziyadah if he had an even chance. The Black, too, had run wild much of his life and he had run to kill other horses. But how would he go with Alec on his back? And was it worth the chance they'd be taking in running over such terrain?

Alec looked up at the great mountain silhouetted against the sky, its peaks mounting like turrets into the stars, and then down at the gardens where hidden floodlights played upon the fishponds and fountains. As he took deep breaths of the cool air, he watched the bats and birds that flew bewilderedly in the glare of the fountain lights. With his eyes he followed the curving jets of water that rose from the mouths of marble lions and tigers, of crocodiles and eagles. He listened to the sound of it falling into green pools, and he thought of Tabari, who had created this enchantment. For whom? Certainly not her husband. For herself then? To keep busy while Abd-al-Rahman sought Ziyadah?

Turning away from the window, Alec stepped from an alcove into the large bedroom. Tabari had furnished it with a brass bed and choice pieces of mahogany furniture that had evidently been imported from England. Scattered over the stone floor were thick, hand-woven rugs of soft colors. A fire burned in the fireplace to take the evening chill from the room, its flames sending a hollow roar up the wide chimney.

A large bathroom, with doors of padded leather, separated Alec's room from Henry's.

Now, as the boy walked into the adjoining room, his friend said, "Put another log on that fire, will you please, Alec?"

Henry, in the pajamas and robe Abd-al-Rahman had loaned him, was already in bed, trying to read. His gray eyes seemed paler and he was shivering.

"Are you all right?" Alec asked anxiously. The room was warm and the top logs in the fireplace were blazing. But he obediently put another log on as Henry had asked.

"Sure, just a little chill. I was thinkin' about being out in that cold last night. I guess that brought it on." He shrugged his shoulders. "Look at me now, stretched out in the lap of luxury." He waved a hand toward his bedside table, which held a steaming tray. "The Sheikh sent Homsi up with chocolate. Have some? There's plenty and he brought an extra cup for you."

"No, thanks," Alec answered. Besides the hot chocolate there were dates, bread and honey. Henry looked very small in the big bed. A table in the center of the room was littered with English racing magazines and it was one of these Henry was reading; its cover showed the Black winning the Brooklyn Handicap.

A chill swept over Alec despite the warmth of the room. To shake it off he took a few turns around the room. The diamond-paned windows, recessed into an alcove like those in his own room, were closed, but he could see the lights of the stable towers.

"I wish I were tired," he said.

"You will be if you get to bed," Henry soothed. "There's no sense worrying any more about it tonight. Tomorrow will be soon enough. We'll think better after a good night's sleep."

Alec remained by the windows, staring out into the night. The face of the stable clock was yellow and dimly lit, its gold hands pointing to ten o'clock. Bats flew within the range of its light and Alec could almost hear the flutter of their wings. He opened the window, not really knowing why he did so, for Henry had said he was cold. But Alec was sure Henry's chill did not come from the night air any more than his own did.

"Do you believe his story?" Alec spoke softly and without changing his position at the windows.

"I guess so — now."

"It's too weird."

"So's life sometimes. What other reason would he have for bein' here if it wasn't to catch Ziyadah?"

"Maybe there's no such horse," Alec suggested. "Not alive, anyway."

"We saw him ourselves ... last night."

"We saw *lights* last night," Alec corrected, "lights and a dim silhouette of what we took to be a horse. But we could have been mistaken."

"We heard hoofbeats."

"I can pound out those, too."

"You're being too skeptical."

"I'm scared of this, Henry. I'm not going to have the Black killed chasing a ghost horse."

"Or yourself either. It's not the Black I'm worried about. He's big and can handle himself. It's you."

"I can handle myself."

"Not if you don't get some sleep."

With the window open Alec could hear the clatter of the stream below. From not too far away came the slap of a rope on rawhide and then a whistle. Three Arab guards came down the stable lane, boots clinking. They walked along the stream and Alec watched them until they had reached the big tent. A fire was blazing before the opening and other Arabs sat around it eating while greyhounds hovered patiently, awaiting scraps of meat and bones. It was a desert scene, wild and beautiful and peaceful.

Why then, if it was so peaceful, did he start at his own shadow? Alec wondered. Why was he filled with all sorts of horrible doubts? As

Henry had said, what other reason would Abd-al-Rahman have for being here if it wasn't to catch a *real, live,* Ziyadah? What was more, wasn't that the reason he and Henry were here too?

His troubled eyes followed the gravel road to the house. Even in the shadows he was able to make out the double flight of stone stairs that led to the front door, with its ponderous bars and bolts. The vast house was a fortress, today as in the past.

No wonder he was not sleepy. The house was getting on his nerves. Despite Tabari's gardens and the modern plumbing and lighting and furniture, the place belonged to the past and to the dead. It was as if Barjas ben Ishak were still alive, walking down the echoing length of his great halls.

Alec shuddered. He glanced at the circular stallion barn that stood on the high knoll across the stream. With the moonlight shining brightly upon its ancient stone, it seemed far more vulnerable to attack than this house. Perhaps, contrary to what he had been told, Barjas ben Ishak had been more afraid of losing his own life than his horses.

Alec closed the window, and Henry said quietly, "Now why don't you go to bed? I'm turning out the light."

The bedside lamp went off but the moon brightened the room. Alec made his way to the foot of Henry's bed. "I — I can't explain the way I feel," he said.

Henry's voice was muffled by the deep pillow. "Y'don't have to. I know."

"I don't think you do. I have a feeling that — "

"We got nothin' to worry about," Henry said sleepily. "Even ghost horses don't bother me none. My big brother used to put me asleep tellin' me the story of the Headless Horseman of Sleepy Hollow. Imagine ridin' pell-mell up an' down the Hudson River on that ol' bag of bones. He wouldn't have lasted a quarter of a mile on a dry track, that one. What a phony!"

With the window shut, the only sound in the room was the roar of the flames sweeping up the chimney. Alec said, "I keep thinking about old Nazar, sitting in front of the barn and waiting through the years for Ziyadah's return."

"He's old. They were humoring him."

"I know, but it took a lot of love to wait that long."

"Maybe they should've had him wait a little longer since Abd-al-Rahman's so sure he's goin' to catch Ziyadah."

Slowly Alec moved across the room. "Good night, Henry."

"Pleasant dreams," Henry said, stifling a yawn.

Alec undressed where he could look out the open window. Some of the mares had been left out and were grazing. The only sounds came from the Arabs sitting around their open fire. As in the desert they would talk until midnight before pulling their sheep-lined outer coverings about them and going to sleep. They were used to solitude, to extreme heat and cold. It was their ancestors who had first mastered the horse and yet had not looked down upon the animal because of it. Instead, they had been indebted to him for *his* friendship, knowing that the horse had reached his physical prime some twenty million years before their race had learned to stand on its feet.

Alec went to bed and closed his eyes to the distant chattering of the Arabs. The moonlight reached out and covered him. From sheer physical exhaustion he fell asleep.

He did not fall immediately into a heavy sleep as would have been expected from one so young and tired. Instead he dozed in fits and spurts, half awake and half asleep, listening for the Arabs and not hearing them. Then it was past midnight and they had gone to sleep. The moonlight moved from his bed, leaving him in deep shadows. He dozed for longer intervals only to wake and listen. For what? A ghost horse?

Listen to the dismal neighing from downwind! It was only the roar from the chimney draft. *Hear the pawing of a horseshoe on stone!* It was the scraping of his bedstead against the stone wall. *Listen to the rush of wings outside his window!* It was the whir of carriage wheels on gravel.

Then came deep silence and he fell heavily asleep. Toward morning he heard the thunder of hoofs. He turned over, refusing to believe them or to be awakened. They seemed to be racing round and round, coming closer and closer, louder and louder. Then his very being was pierced by the Black's shrill scream, followed by the blast of another stallion! Yet when he jumped out of bed there was nothing to be heard but the far-off sound of running hoofs and the high, wavering whinnies of the mares.

It was the hour before dawn and the waning moon was partly obscured by a thin veil of mist. Alec stood at the window with not a muscle moving. As if in a hypnotic spell, his eyes were fixed on a shimmering stream of sparks moving beyond the end wall. Yet only a few moments ago Ziyadah must have been within the fenced fields! Alec had only to listen to the stabled Black and the excited mares to be certain of this.

He felt a nameless terror grow within him, as on the previous night when he had first seen this fiery spectacle. He watched the trail of sparks rise into the jagged mountain vastnesses where there was nothing but sheer rock. He leaned out the window, wanting to breathe the cold air and rid himself of his terror.

"It is Ziyadah, a stallion of flesh and blood," he said aloud. "Moonlight and shadows are playing tricks with my eyes. He's finding cracks and crevices and roots for a foothold. Listen to the Black screaming in his stall! He knows, too, that it's no ghost horse. He wants to fight."

The sparks became a single red glow which floated rather than moved, descending into the depths either of the night or some abyss, then suddenly emerging into flight again. Perspiration broke out over Alec. Where was everybody? Where were the lanterns of the Arab guards? Where was Henry? He waited until the glowing light faded on a distant peak, then he went to a chair and sat down. He must not think of ghost horses and magic and wizards. He must...

There was a pounding upon his door. "Alec! Alec!" The voice was Abd-al-Rahman's.

"I'm coming." Alec's steps were slow, his feet

leaden. Abd-al-Rahman was already dressed.

"Come along!" the Sheikh said, his dark eyes bright. "We can still pick up his tracks. Hurry!"

"But Henry . . ."

"He's sleeping. Let him be. We ride alone!"

Alec pulled on his clothes quickly. The Sheikh was right. Why drag poor Henry out at this hour?

A few minutes later Alec was outside and walking with Abd-al-Rahman toward the stables. The night was cold and dark with the moon gone. But it wasn't still. There were movements in the great house behind the dimly lit windows. The Arabs were up and talking excitedly. Dogs barked incessantly and from the stables came shouts and whistles and neighs.

Abd-al-Rahman strode silently a little ahead of Alec. He was dressed in the same camel's hair breeches and short jacket he had worn earlier in the evening. Strapped to his hip was a revolver in a black leather case. Alec checked the question that rose to his lips, but of one thing he was sure: One did not track ghosts with a gun.

Leaving Abd-al-Rahman at the stables, Alec climbed the knoll to the stallion barn. He heard the Black's constant pawing behind the closed wooden door and spoke to him as he opened it. Eager to get out, the stallion pushed hard against him while Alec slipped the halter over his ears and whispered, "Maybe you'll have a chance to show your sire how bright a desert star can be!"

Alec led the black stallion to the stableyard where Abd-al-Rahman awaited him. The Sheikh stood beside a sleek gray mare with a camel's hair halter and a light saddle pad. There was a ring at the back of the noseband which could be tightened to act as a bit. But where, Alec wondered, were the rich bridles of feathers and ostrich plumes which he remembered from Arabia? And the tassels and saddles of vivid colors?

Noting the boy's scrutiny of his horse's tack, Abd-al-Rahman said, "I dress my mares to please myself. And you? Can I supply you with the same?" He held up the woven shank that was attached to the mare's noseband.

"We're all right," Alec said, mounting his horse from a block. He pressed his hands and legs upon the black hide and the stallion jumped.

The stable clock said five o'clock as they rode off into the darkness. Only once did the Black attempt to bolt, and even then Alec had no difficulty in controlling him. For the rest of the way to the main gate Alec kept his horse behind Abd-al-Rahman's, noting the new authority in the set of the Sheikh's head and shoulders.

"Where were your guards when he came?" Alec asked.

"They were not alert."

"They didn't even see him?"

"Not close and not until too late. They had been dozing," the Sheikh said contemptuously. His voice promised that he would deal with them later. Dismounting at the gate, he opened it with a large brass key.

"Then they didn't see how he got in and out?"

"They say they were blinded by the fire from his hoofs but they believe he jumped as he approached this wall. They are, of course, lying to cover their own carelessness. It has withstood the attack of armies. He could not have jumped over it."

"If he did, he could jump over the moon," Alec said.

"He is no ghost," Abd-al-Rahman insisted, locking the gate after Alec had ridden through and mounting his sleek mare. "There has to be a way he comes and goes."

They left the road to cross the rolling fields that stretched to the base of the mountain. It was here Alec had seen the horse from his window. There must be some mark of his hoofs, some evidence of the path he had taken.

They rode slowly, awaiting the swift approach of day and saving their horses until they needed them most. There was no separateness of thought in the two riders now. They hunted as one, their hands and legs speaking the same commands to their mounts while their eyes searched the ground before them. The sun rose but it did not reach the chilled slopes of the mountain where they searched. Both were sure that it was here Ziyadah had run.

Alec eased the Black carefully through a rough sidehill. If Ziyadah had gone before them, why wasn't there a hoofprint to be seen, or even a scratch on stone? Ziyadah had been running so there should be many such marks from his hoofs.

A cloud crossed the sun and the early morning darkened. A chill swept over Alec as the wind came sighing down from the mountain tops. The Black's nostrils flared but he did not sound forth his challenge. He scented no other stallion.

Abd-al-Rahman's sharp eyes read the ground as easily as the pages of a book, yet they found nothing. Ziyadah was gone and so were his tracks, *if he'd left any*. But of course he had, Alec told himself. They'd find a mark of some kind, somewhere. No horse was able to vanish into thin air!

The minutes stretched into long hours and their trained eyes found nothing. They rode until they could ride no farther, for the mountain wall rose sheer and impassable above them. They turned their horses, retracing their path and starting over again, spreading out this time in order to make sure of missing no stone or patch of ground where Ziyadah might have left a track. Still they found no sign of his passing.

They went back to try again and again, taking their horses step by step along the mountain slope, until their eyes grew tired from the constant strain and they were forced to stop. They turned homeward in the twilight with Alec doubting he'd even seen a horse the night before. The search for Ziyadah had ended without his even having taken the Black out of a walk.

15 BLACK HOURS

Alec learned that he had not reckoned fully
with the set of Abd-al-Rahman's head and
shoulders or the hawk's glint in his eyes. He
found that the search for Ziyadah had only
begun. That night, hidden behind the trees,
their horses tied and waiting, he and the Sheikh
awaited Ziyadah's return to the mares. Others
too watched for the lone stallion's coming, and
signals had been arranged that would send the
Black and Alec out after him. Nothing happened.

The next day they rode alone again, for Abd-
al-Rahman would not let Henry accompany
them.

"The way is dangerous," he said. "It is enough that we risk the legs of two fine horses."

Henry grunted. "To say nothing of two guys' necks." He did not attempt to force the issue, for he, too, saw the look in the Sheikh's eyes and the gun strapped to his hip.

Day followed day while Alec rode the Black through the wildest country he'd ever seen, dropping into deep canyons and climbing the sweep of the mountainsides. Nothing moved except the wind. Nothing was heard but the wind. There was no sign of Ziyadah. Not a click or clatter or scratch of his hoofs. Alec grew impatient and on the fourth day he told Abd-al-Rahman, "I'd like to give up the ghost. My horse is stiffening up from this kind of going."

The Sheikh led the way down a ragged bluff, his mare almost sitting on her hindquarters to keep her balance. Alec had no choice but to follow. "Easy," he said to his horse. The Black slid down the embankment by gathering up his hind legs and bending them under his body, then bracing his forelegs as he let himself go down.

At the base of the bluff Abd-al-Rahman said, "He's here somewhere, waiting for us to come upon him. Then you shall have your race, you and the Black!" The Sheikh's eyes searched the changing shapes of the shadows on the broken slopes above them.

Alec said nothing. What if they saw Ziyadah and couldn't run him down? After all, he wasn't going to send the Black at top speed through this kind of country! Not for Abd-al-Rahman or anyone else.

Alec's impatience grew with the hours while they searched for ways that would enable them to climb the mountain. He listened to the Black's breathing and the scuff of his hoofs on stone and wondered when the Sheikh would call a halt to this futile quest. He was tired of looking at Abd-al-Rahman's clamped jaws, tired of the search and, like his horse, just plain tired. His impatience turned to anger.

"If Ziyadah means so much to you, why didn't you keep his colts?" he asked almost defiantly.

The bearded face did not turn toward Alec, nor did the dark eyes give up their search of the crags and ridges. "None of them had his speed," he said.

"How do you know?"

"It is my business to know such things. I tried them. No, the mares were not right for Ziyadah."

"Why did you send them to the States?"

"Where else do they pay such high prices for yearlings?"

"You're not poor," Alec said.

"On the contrary, Alec. Between us, Tabari and I are very rich." He smiled for the first time. "But we are Bedouins as well. We could not resist such easy plunder."

"So you went to all the trouble of —"

"But it was no trouble at all, Alec," Abd-al-Rahman interrupted. "It was my old school friend Angel who did all the work. He came with his plane and took the colts to America. He made arrangements with the agent there. I had little to do with it. But Angel was well paid, and it is he who needs money for his bulls and that ridiculous game he plays on horseback."

"At least it's an honest game," Alec retorted.

Abd-al-Rahman smiled. "You have grown longer spurs since our last meeting in Arabia, Alec. You are a fighting cock now and crowing. It is as Tabari said months ago . . . our colts would not pass your eye without your guessing their sire. She said you would track us down, even here. I answered, 'Let him come, for he will not travel without the Black and with such a horse we may catch Ziyadah!' And so it is at this moment."

"So it is," Alec repeated quietly.

"All but my taking Ziyadah," the Sheikh reminded. "Come, let us see if that too cannot be arranged. There is still a half day before us."

They descended into a dark canyon, overspread with long shadows and a dry stream bed. Crossing it, they rode beneath the jagged rock formation of an overhanging cliff. They found a break in the rock and climbed again, moving higher and higher onto a humped ridge. All the while their eyes searched the towering mountain, seeking some way to surmount it as Ziyadah must have done. But as on preceding days they finally reached an end to the trail. The path they had chosen stopped before a wall of sheer stone. Hours later, they turned their horses homeward, little knowing that the long, tedious search for Ziyadah temporarily had come to an end.

As they approached the stables, Abd-al-Rahman kicked his gray mare into a run.

"What's up?" Alec asked, the Black running easily beside the gray mare.

"Tabari is back."

"How can you tell?"

"The mares. See how they have gathered near the house. They do it only when she is home."

"Does she feed them?"

"Occasionally, but it is much more than that.

Often they will spend hours there as if they wanted nothing more than for her to look upon them. It is strange too that they know when she is home even though they cannot see her."

Abd-al-Rahman spoke hurriedly and his eyes showed his impatience to be with his wife. He spurred his mare. Alec, not wanting to run the Black all the way to the stables, did not follow. When Abd-al-Rahman arrived at the house, Homsi appeared as if by magic and led the gray mare away. The Sheikh ran up the long flight of steps, taking several at a time.

It was an hour later when Alec approached the house, having taken care of his horse for the night. He glanced at the mares gathered in the field just beyond the gardens. They were standing still, their small heads turned in the direction of the house, and neighing occasionally. Alec was not surprised that they knew of Tabari's being home even though they could not see her. Scent was the most highly developed faculty of a horse and if she fed them any tidbits it was only natural for them to connect some scent with her presence. Strangely enough the Black, too, had turned toward the house when they had passed it.

The front door opened before Alec had a chance to reach for the brass handle. The liveried footman said, "If it is convenient, Madam would like to see you."

Tabari was alone. She sat in a high-backed, carved wooden chair looking out the window at the mares. Beside her on a small table were pastries and a pot of tea.

She spoke without turning her head. "Sometimes I sit here for hours just watching them."

"Don't you ride any more?" Alec wanted to know.

"No. It is their movements I enjoy most of all now. It is like watching a fine ballet."

"He would not have liked it this way," Alec said, referring to her father.

"Perhaps not."

"His death was an accident. Don't you see? It could have happened to anyone."

"Would you care for tea?" Her tone was gracious, her manner polite.

"No, thank you." Suddenly Alec was conscious of his dusty clothes and dirty hands. "I'd better clean up."

"Please stay a few minutes. It is good talking to you again." She was friendly yet her voice was commanding.

"If you like." He was aware of the subtle but heady perfume she wore. It was an easy scent for the mares to catch. "Did you have a good trip?" he asked.

"Yes, except for strong headwinds coming back." She rose from the chair, her figure as slim and pliable as a willow reed.

"Do you keep your plane where we landed with González?"

"Of course. There is no other level field in these mountains. Did you not notice our hangar against the west wall?"

"No, we didn't. It wasn't much of a morning."

She sauntered to the window and for a short while was silent. Then she asked curiously, "How long have you been searching for Ziyadah?"

"Four days I think it is now . . . and some nights. I've lost track. Your husband would know."

She stood quietly in front of the window, her raven-black hair shining brilliantly in the rays cast by the setting sun, her hands remaining deep in the pockets of her blue skirt. "It is ridiculous," she said at last.

"Then you don't think we have a chance of catching him?" Alec saw the sudden scorn in her eyes and was almost glad. Only she could influence Abd-al-Rahman to call off this search. Even if it were only for a short time, a rest would be welcome.

In answer Tabari went to a large desk and withdrew an envelope. She straightened up, her eyes flashing, and said, "This is my father's written statement that the skeleton found by the mountaineers was that of Ziyadah."

"No one knew horses better than your father. If he said Ziyadah is dead, he's dead. But . . ."

Alec was aware of her sudden receptiveness. As she crossed the room toward him, her eyes held a faraway look. For the first time since the plane had landed him in this wild country Alec felt close to her, and he was reminded of the friendship they'd shared in the desert.

She said in a low voice, her face flushed, "My father came to me one day in this very room and said, *'Daughter, mark this hour well for the colt of colts has been foaled!'* "

"And it was Ziyadah?"

She nodded. "Oh, Alec, this foal was no different from the others in the beginning. His way of going was the same, his legs were no longer, his bones no stronger. But as a yearling he became everything my father had foretold. Ziyadah was not a big colt, which was a surprise even to my father, but he was a very fountain of speed and vitality! He was all fire and none of the other horses would dare play with him for fear of incurring his wrath!"

For a few seconds she paused. Then she went on. "Has my husband told you that Ziyadah's coat was of burnished copper, so highly polished that it returned the sun's rays as would a mirror?"

Alec shook his head.

"It was the color of the ancient stones used by my ancestors to build this fortress," she said, her eyes suddenly clouding. "My father believed that this too proclaimed Ziyadah as the brightest star of the desert, the one who had been sought by our people for so many generations. He looked forward to the day when Ziyadah would prove that he could pass on his speed, stamina and heart to his first colt."

Her back suddenly stiffened and she turned abruptly away from him. "You know the rest," she concluded bitterly. "It was this colt — now your Black — who killed him."

For many minutes a heavy silence filled the room broken only by the flapping of wings against the upper panes of the window.

Tabari said, "Probably a pigeon." She tried to assume an air of lightness but there was fear in her eyes.

Their gazes met and Alec for some reason felt cold. But all that Tabari said was, "Since Ziyadah is truly dead you and my husband are only wasting your time."

"I wish you'd tell him that," Alec said.

"You cannot catch a *ghost*."

Alec attempted a smile but it faded fast. "I don't believe in ghosts," he said.

"But I do." She spoke with intensity, in a voice barely above a whisper. *"For I have found a hoofprint made by no earthly horse."*

16 BLACK HUNTER

Alec, sitting in the tub, allowed the water to rise until it had almost reached his neck before he turned it off. His muscles were sore, for he wasn't used to riding over such rough terrain as he had encountered here. The water felt good and he closed his eyes, trying not to listen to Henry's long tirade coming from the next room.

"I tell you, Alec, we're goin' to get out of here someway! It's not the Black I'm worried about, but you. This guy will kill you off for sure. You're no judge of this kind of riding. You make one mistake in these mountains and you're done. I told that to Abd an' I'm goin' to tell him again! Either he quits this night-and-day search for Ziyadah or we clear out of here — and make no bones about it!

"I've been talkin' to some of these gardeners. Not that we understand each other's lingo but they have an idea what I'm after. They hold up the fingers of both hands five times when I ask them how far it is to their village. An' they point to the south, past the field where we landed. I figure they mean it's fifty miles that way. All we got to do is to get a few cans of grub, give the Black his head to the south an' go. With his keen scent we'll find our way all right. We're no fools. Why, from the way this fellow's driving you ..."

Tabari had said the hoofprint she had found was stubby rather than oval-shaped; it was thick and short but unquestionably that of a horse's hoof. More ghostly still, there was only one. She had seen it when Jason had stopped the carriage horses for a breather coming home. It was in the soft bank of a mountain stream and fresh, made no longer ago than last night!

A little later Alec dressed in fresh clothes loaned to him by Abd-al-Rahman.

Tabari had said she wasn't going to tell her husband of the strange hoofprint. She wanted him to stay home with her.

Henry joined Alec and began striding up and

down the room making plans for their departure.

Alec thought only of the hoofprint. His bath had refreshed him and he believed in ghost horses less than ever. If there was a hoofprint it had been made by a real horse. If there was one track there had to be others. They would be fresh, made only last night, and easy to follow.

Alec and Henry left the room for dinner and walked down the long hall, their steps echoing the full length of it. Near the stairs they came to a halt for Abd-al-Rahman's bedroom door was open and he called them inside.

"We'll go down together," he said, while waiting for Homsi to bring his coat from a large wardrobe cabinet. His appearance was out of keeping with the herd rider they had come to know. He wore a white linen suit and his black patent-leather shoes were brilliantly polished. His beard, too, had been trimmed. He smiled at them while glancing toward the open door of the adjoining room.

"I'll tell Tabari we'll meet her downstairs," he said. "She'll be a little late, I'm afraid."

They saw Tabari sitting before the mirror of a dressing table, brushing her black hair. Abd-al-Rahman went to her and said something, taking one of her hands and enclosing it in his. When he turned around his eyes could not conceal his sheer adoration for his wife.

168

Alec had no doubt that Abd-al-Rahman would call off the search temporarily just as Tabari wanted. He noted the bright Arabian blankets on the bed and the yellow-and-black tanned skins of mountain lion and bear which covered the floor. It was a man's room, the room of a hunter, in contrast to the adjoining room, which was as soft and feminine as Tabari.

He heard his hostess call his name.

"Alec," she said, "he has promised not to ride tonight. Now you will have your rest." She was leaning back in her chair, her eyes bright and dancing.

"We'll leave that up to Alec, my dear," Abd-al-Rahman corrected her gently.

Alec glanced at the Sheikh questioningly. From the young and powerful hunter he had become a schoolboy who was very eager to please.

Tabari's face darkened. "But you promised," she said in a peevish tone.

"I said only that *I* planned to stay home with you. Alec can do as he wishes. He might like to ride alone." Abd-al-Rahman turned from his wife to Alec, his expression one of slight annoyance. "I didn't realize I was pressing you so hard. Tabari seems to think — "

"I told her only that I was tired," Alec said.

"And he has every right to be!" Henry interjected angrily. "What mad plans do you have for him anyway?"

The blood rushed to the Shiekh's face. "I plan nothing for Alec that he doesn't want to do himself!" he said in a clipped voice. "Now enough of this!" Picking up his key ring from the dresser, he shoved it angrily into his pants' pocket.

Alec said, "I guess I will ride tonight. I'd sort of figured on it." Actually, he hadn't decided until that very moment.

They all turned upon him and Henry was the first to speak. "Say that again, Alec."

"I'm riding. There's something I've got to find out." Alec paused, refusing to meet Henry's eyes. "It won't take long." He turned to Abd-al-Rahman. "I'll need the key to the outer gate."

"You're sure you want to go alone? I can send someone with you, perhaps Homsi. There's no better rider."

"I'm the one who's goin' along," Henry said insistently.

"No, I'd better go alone," Alec answered. "I'll work faster that way and get back sooner."

The Shiekh handed Alec a large key from the ring. "Good hunting!" he said, smiling at his wife.

Tabari shook her head, and in a far corner of

the room where it was semi-dark, Homsi's eyes glowed as yellow as a cat's.

Later that night Alec rode the Black past the house, the lights looming bright against the mountain. He sent his horse into an easy lope, and the four black hoofs beat out a quiet cadence. He watched the stallion's ears and listened to the wind sighing across the land. He felt as if he owned the world. It was always that way when he was alone, riding the Black.

A shaft of light split the darkness near by where the mares grazed. The guards were alert. Alec took the Black to the side of the drive, the soft earth muffling the sound of the stallion's hoofs. Soon they'd leave the pastures and guards behind. The wind, sweeping up from the south, became a little stronger. It rippled the tall grass and made the trees creak as branches scratched against each other. Alec hoped it wouldn't rain.

As the Black warmed to his work Alec eased him into a faster, long, swinging lope. The grass was fine for running, not too hard and not too soft, and the stallion wanted to be let out even more. He snorted constantly and shifted into greater speeds whenever Alec relaxed his hold.

"Not now," Alec told him. He must save the Black's speed and stamina. He must watch out for him every minute, especially later on. It was strange to think that such a powerful horse needed protection. But Alec knew the Black would run for him until he died, would work until he dropped . . . so he needed a champion.

Despite Alec's soft words and hands, the Black quickened his strides, his hoofs sounding like thunder. It swelled to a roar and the south wind whistled. Only when they neared the high wall did the stallion's strides shorten and his speed lessen. He came to a stop readily as if his desire to run free had temporarily been satisfied.

Alec opened the big gate with the key Abd-al-Rahman had given him. He said to his horse, "I only hope you've saved something in case we meet up with Ziyadah. If you haven't, it won't be much of a race."

He led the Black away from the road. He did not feel fearless or bold, only prepared to do his best. He knew what he and his horse could do. His eyes and ears were alert, his seat balanced. He knew where he was going.

He sent the Black into a lope and felt the drive of the black legs under him. Swerving into the brush, he slowed the stallion to a walk and guided him down a moderate slope, the shortest way to the stream Tabari had mentioned. Suddenly the Black came to an abrupt halt, pricking up his ears and whistling. Alec was startled, for his horse seemed attracted by something on the slope above. Alec, too, looked up. He sensed movement but at first saw nothing. Finally he saw it, a white patch on a fawn-colored rump. "Move on," he said to the Black. "It's only a deer. We have more than that to look for."

When they were back on the road again Alec saw the fresh tracks of the carriage. He found the exact spot where, as Tabari had said, they'd stopped to rest the horses. The mud was thick beside the stream and he had no trouble finding the strange hoofprint. It was like none he'd ever seen before, too short and thick, too stubby. And yet he had no doubt that it had been made by a horse. He walked up and down the stream, searching for other prints but found none. Was Tabari right? Was this no earthly horse they sought? He found himself listening for the plop-plop of ghostly hoofs in the mud.

After a while he mounted the Black and rode into the brush. A fine mist was now being borne on the southerly wind. It drifted about him and his horse, making him feel very much alone. Suddenly he raised his hands and the Black came to a stop. Alec slid off the black horse and ran a few feet into the brush. There he bent down to observe some horse droppings. They were warm.

Looking up into the mist, he whispered,

"We're not alone then, black horse. And it's no ghost that's watching us. He's up there where you can't catch his scent. Listen for him. He won't keep quiet long."

Alec mounted and the wind swept the black mane into his face. *"Go slow,"* he told his horse. The long legs moved beneath him. *"You won't need to use all your speed. Remember that. Don't use it all. Be ready to stop and turn and jump. It'll be that kind of a race. We want to corner him if we can but we don't want to kill ourselves doing it."*

There was a sudden movement to the Black's ears. Then he whistled a short, sharp blast.

Alec looked wildly around. Less than a hundred yards above them a small, bright spark glittered in the night, disappeared, then showed again in the same spot. Had it been made by a pawing, plated hoof striking stone?

Alec felt the Black's sinewy legs quicken stride. "No," he whispered to his horse, "not yet. Go slow. Save yourself."

Suddenly the whistle of another stallion pierced the silent air. The Black jumped, throwing Alec forward so that his chin was buried in the flying mane. Alec rocked back as the stallion swerved about some brush, closing in rapidly upon the spot from where the sparks had come. *Ziyadah!*

The moon had broken through the swift-moving clouds and Alec made out the silhouette of a running horse. He had no doubt that it was Ziyadah for the horse ran with the agility of one who knew every inch of the terrain. Like a flying cloak trailed the shimmering streak of blue and red and orange lights which Alec had seen twice before. It was these weird lights Alec followed, his blood racing in his excitement and the thrill of so close a chase. Their speed was dangerous and he knew that a fall meant certain death, but he had confidence in his horse's sure strides. Where Ziyadah went the Black could go too!

The wind whipped the air away from Alec and it became hard for him to breathe. Sight of the other stallion had aroused the Black and he ran wildly, swerving around brush and rocks at lightning speed.

They were not overtaking Ziyadah but on the other hand he was not drawing away. So long as they didn't lose him Alec felt confident they'd run him down.

"Don't use up all you've got," he kept repeating to the Black. *"Save something. He's afraid or he'd turn and fight. He can't shake us off. Stay with him."*

They had only a short distance to go before reaching the vast wall of rock which had stopped Alec and Abd-al-Rahman so often before. Would it halt Ziyadah's wild run? Would this be the end of the chase?

They entered the darker-than-night shadows of the mountain and the wall of rock towered above them. There was no slowing of the trail of sparks nor did the Black's strides slacken. The tall stallion swerved with the twisting, rocky path, and Alec could not tell if this was one of the approaches they had attempted previously or not.

Suddenly he saw the sparks swing upward as if Ziyadah had swerved and then taken a tremendous bound into the air! Startled and uncertain, Alec reached for the Black's halter to slow him down. But quickly he let go, giving the stallion his head. Better now to trust the Black's judgment than his own! He regained his balance as the Black swerved, following the sparks. Alec barely had time to get a good grip with his legs when the stallion jumped.

The Black took in the situation before Alec did. He was in midair and flying over a low wall when he sensed danger. Suddenly he changed the direction of his leap by twisting his body to one side. Alec bent his head low over the Black's neck as the wrenching of the great body almost tore his arms out of their sockets. With folded hocks beneath his quarters and extended forelegs, the Black landed at an angle on the other side of the wall, his body scraping stone. He lurched forward, regained his balance, but didn't go on, for his right hind leg had slipped between *two cut pieces of hard sprucewood and was held fast!* He made one attempt to break free and when he failed he stood perfectly still, awaiting Alec's help.

Alec slid off his shaking horse, fury welling up within him when he saw the *man-made* trap that had been set for them. He removed the big stones that held down the long slats at both ends. Beneath them was a hole just deep enough to cause serious injury to any horse. Fortunately, except for one hoof the Black had avoided the trap.

Alec looked up, following Ziyadah's fiery trail as the horse climbed the mountain. He wasn't going to follow him any longer . . . at least, not tonight. Furious as he was, he might make a mistake, and he and the Black might not be allowed another chance. His body trembled in his anger and hot tears ran down his cheeks.

Who had set this deadly trap?

17 BLACK EYES

The light of early morning came through the diamond-paned windows. "You should have woke me," Henry said. "I slept in the chair, sure I'd hear the racket of those door bolts when they let you in."

"What difference would it have made?"

"We could have found out who was in the house and who *wasn't!*" Henry exploded.

Alec shook his head, tucking in his shirt tail. "The trap could have been set earlier."

"Then someone is pretty well acquainted with Ziyadah's ways," Henry said.

"Of course," Alec answered. He pulled his belt tight and squared his shoulders. "And I aim to find out who it is. I'm going to follow Ziyadah's trail up the mountain."

"No you're not," Henry said quietly. There was a new note to his voice that meant business.

"Why not?"

Henry went to a chair and sat down. At any other time he would have liked the strong set of Alec's jaw and shoulders. "Have you considered why somebody should want to set such a trap?"

"To keep Ziyadah from being caught," Alec replied.

"I don't think so," Henry said, his face darkening. "Why would anyone in this house want to hide Ziyadah in the mountains? Can you think of an answer?"

Alec went to the window. "Maybe it isn't anyone in this house," he answered quietly.

"Who else then?" Henry rose from his chair and went to the boy, clamping a hand firmly on his shoulder. "I don't think Ziyadah's appearance last night was accidental, Alec. I believe it was all planned, including your chasing him. The trap was set for *you*."

Alec turned to his friend. "But ... why?"

"I don't know the answer to that," Henry said, beginning to pace the floor, "but it's the reason I'm keeping you from riding again."

Alec was silent, stunned by Henry's words.

Why would anyone want to kill him? He had no enemies.

"The whole business of our bein' here is weird and yet almost as if it was carefully planned," Henry said, meeting the boy's eyes. "They figured on our comin'. Abd-al-Rahman told us that." He paused. "I wonder if it's the Black he's after. With you out of the way and then me . . ."

"I don't believe that," Alec said. "No man would kill for a horse . . . any horse, even the Black."

"You're mistaken about that," Henry said. "Remember the stories we've heard of Bedouins fightin' wars for fast horses."

"Not Abd-al-Rahman," Alec said, but like his voice the expression on his face was indecisive.

"Blood runs deep, especially Bedouin blood when there's a horse concerned," Henry reminded him.

Alec shook his head. "Abd-al-Rahman could have gotten rid of us long before this if he'd wanted to."

"Not and have it look accidental," Henry pointed out, "like a fall from a horse."

Alec put on his shoes. He thought of another night, when a lone bull had come out of the darkness to attack him. Had that, too, been accidental? He got up and went to the door.

"Where are you going?" Henry asked.

"To feed and rub him down. His leg is all right but needs attention."

"I'll go with you," the trainer offered.

"All right," Alec said. "I wanted to tell you something anyway . . . something that happened that first night at Angel González'. I went to the big bull pasture . . ." The padded leather door closed behind them.

It was six o'clock by the stableyard clock when they reached the stallion barn.

"Then Angel González could be mixed up in this dirty business more than we figured," Henry said when Alec had finished his story of the lone bull. "I'm not exactly surprised."

The Black reached for the grain as Alec poured it into the feed box. Kneeling in the straw, the boy felt the stallion's right hind leg and found it cool without any noticeable swelling. Nevertheless he began rubbing it with a leg liniment he'd found in the tack room. It had a strong, sharp smell that smarted his eyes and nose.

Henry said, "I want you to keep quiet about what happened. Tell them you saw nothing."

"Why?"

"Only one person will know we're lyin'. Maybe he'll give himself away."

"All right," Alec agreed. "We'll try it your way. It's easier than climbing mountains."

"And a lot less dangerous."

They went to breakfast totally unprepared for the shock of seeing Don Angel Rafael González sitting at the table. Behind him hovered the old woman María, her heavy body wobbling from side to side as she passed the hot dishes.

"Good morning! Good morning!" González boomed, rising to greet them. "We meet again under far more pleasant conditions, eh, my friends?"

"At least the sun's shining," Henry said bitterly, recovering before Alec did.

Abd-al-Rahman sat at the head of the table with Tabari on his right. Behind them stood Homsi.

Tabari said, "Then you did not hear their plane last evening? Ah, but it was very late and you were sleeping heavily. Tell us, Alec, how was your hunt?"

Before answering, Alec turned to those sitting at the long table — to Abd-al-Rahman, who had stiffened in his chair, looking every inch the hard desert hunter he was — to Tabari with the arched smile on her lips — to Angel González, who was helping himself to more eggs and meat — to María, who stood behind him, more mother than servant, pouring hot milk into González' big coffee cup — and finally to Homsi, whose frail body could hardly be seen behind Abd-al-Rahman's chair.

"Not very successful," Alec replied at last in answer to Tabari's question. As far as he could tell there was absolutely no change of expression on the face of any of his listeners.

González was the first to speak. He shrugged his big shoulders gracefully and said, "You hear, María? You have been worrying needlessly about our young friend. He goes hunting alone at night! He is very brave."

"I know that well," she said quietly, "and so should you. Did he not save your life?"

"And I shall be forever grateful!" González said, turning to Alec and smiling.

"A nice way you had of showing it," Henry interjected. "Leaving us like you did."

The big man shrugged his shoulders again. "I did not think it so bad at the time. I was eager to return home and thought your wait would be but a short one. It was María who took me to task for leaving you as I did. She was furious. She insisted upon our coming back and finally I consented." He turned toward Abd-al-Rahman. "We are here," he concluded, "to make sure they arrived safely in your home."

The young Sheikh smiled graciously. "We can still conduct business," he said. "Your trip has not been for nothing."

"Yes, there is always business," González agreed.

"Perhaps when it's done we can fly back with

you," Henry suggested, trying to conceal his eagerness.

The big man's scowl deepened the long scar across his cheek. "Of course," he said, "it is perfectly all right with me." He turned to Abd-al-Rahman, his eyes questioning.

Homsi's face was a mask of cold scorn. Tabari's sandaled feet scraped the bare floor. María's heavy lids lifted, disclosing the keen interest she, too, had in the Sheikh's answer.

"Alec and Henry are free to go whenever they please," Abd-al-Rahman said kindly, although his eyes belied his gracious manner. "It is they who have given up the search for Ziyadah, *not I*!"

Henry pretended to eat, while speaking softly to Alec. "Keep your eyes down and keep still. All he's got to do is to look at you to know you've got the wind up about something. Let me handle it."

González had sat back in his chair and was patting his big stomach. He said with feigned casualness, hoping to relieve the tension that had descended upon the room, "It is all muscle, like a bull's."

Henry turned to Abd-al-Rahman again. "Will your business with González take long?" It was impossible for him to read anything in the Sheikh's set face.

"Only a few hours," Abd-al-Rahman answered finally.

"Then . . ." Henry turned back to González and found that the big man's cheek had begun twitching.

"We'll leave tomorrow morning," González said.

María shifted her big bulk and nodded her gray head approvingly. She poured more scalding milk into González' cup.

Abd-al-Rahman's face darkened despite Tabari's quick movement of a hand on his arm. He fixed piercing eyes upon Alec as he said scornfully, "*Afferin!* You came here crowing like a young cock. Now you run like a jackal! Go home and take your black stud who knows nothing but soft tracks that are kind to his feet!"

The Sheikh rose from his chair, shaking off Tabari's hand. Taking his brass key ring from his pocket, he flung it across the table and it slid into Alec's lap. "Play everything safe, my young friend. Lock up your black treasure so he will not disappear like Ziyadah! Close yourself up within these fortress walls! Flee tomorrow to your safe, soft, and comfortable world! Leave me to find Ziyadah alone. You are not worthy of such a chase!"

"Easy, Alec," Henry said aloud, for the boy's

face was pinched and white. "Keep your eyes down."

The Sheikh angrily left the room.

Tabari was the first to break the silence that followed. She tried to make light of her husband's furious outburst. "He's like a little boy sometimes," she said. "He wants to play *Follow the Leader* and always be the leader. You, Alec, have spoiled the game for him. He wanted you to follow him after Ziyadah."

Alec looked at her and said, "I can't agree with you, Tabari. I don't think he's ever been the little boy you claim him to be. He's rough and tough and hard beneath all the polish you've tried to give him. He'll get what he wants, *even Ziyadah*."

She didn't answer but fear showed in her eyes as she left the room.

18 BLACK ROOM

That evening Alec and Henry were the only ones at dinner. Afterward they went to the living room, where they found Tabari standing in front of the roaring flames in the fireplace.

"Where's everybody?" Henry asked, trying to appear casual.

She turned around and appraised him. Finally she smiled as if deciding that she too would pretend nothing had happened that morning. "I believe they're still talking business," she said lightly. "Angel is very anxious, it seems, to get more yearlings to sell in the United States."

"They brought good prices, then?" Henry asked.

"*Very* good, I understand. But I'm afraid he won't get any more like the ones he had. Not unless Ziyadah is caught."

"I thought you believed Ziyadah to be a *ghost* horse," Alec said quietly.

"Isn't he?" she asked, smiling as she lowered herself into a chair.

"Not if you believe he sired the Sales yearlings."

"I'm only guessing," she answered. "Really, Alec, you never joke at all."

Henry had begun pacing the large living room, winding his way around furniture that was beautiful and polished with age. "The point is, do you think he's goin' to let us go tomorrow?" he asked, coming to a stop before Tabari.

"Of course. Why not? He is a man of his word."

Her gaze shifted to Alec, who was nervously toying with the key ring Abd-al-Rahman had given him that morning. "Did you lock your horse's stall?" she asked, her brows arched.

Alec nodded in embarrassment. "Not that I was afraid anything would happen to him," he said lamely.

She looked at him as if they were the only two persons in the room. "I know," she said evenly, "and you'd better leave him there for the night. No more hunting."

Henry bumped into a couch. "He's goin' nowhere but to bed," he promised.

Tabari rose from her chair and went to the fireplace. Her walk and manner were casual but she said with sudden coldness, "You have made my husband more determined than ever to capture Ziyadah. He is a fool running after folly!"

Henry said, "You'd better not let him hear you say that because first of all he's a *horseman.*"

She whirled upon him, her eyes still cold and steady. "You men are all alike," she said evenly. "And the more I watch you work with horses the less I believe you know anything about the treatment of them under heavy strain. Only my father . . ." Suddenly all the vitality left her and she appeared tired and lonely as she went on, ". . . he could put iron in their bodies and fire in their spirits."

"A big order," Henry said. He didn't like the contemptuous, half-pitying look she had for him. "I've found a horse either has it or doesn't have it. A good trainer simply tries to get the best out of him."

She stamped a small foot on the floor to add emphasis to her words. "*You* race your horses on flat tracks with well rounded turns!" she said in a loud, clear voice. "Only great trainers and great horses know what it is to race over rough, uneven ground where jumps are hard and landings harder. Those are the kind of horses my father raised!"

Henry's face was flaming red and he didn't try to keep the anger out of his voice. "There are easier ways to ruin a horse than to rip its muscles and split its bones by racin' over that kind of going!"

Alec stepped between them, sorry for Tabari because he realized more than Henry how much she had adored her father. It was her deep grief for his loss that made her say things she didn't really mean. Actually, Abu Ishak had been more interested in speed than jumping ability — and Tabari knew that as well as he did.

The door to the room opened and Abd-al-Rahman walked in followed by Angel González. Tabari glanced swiftly at her husband and the somber, grief-stricken look disappeared from her eyes. In its place appeared a radiance that filled the room. She laughed lightly and clapped her hands with all the gaiety of a little girl. With easy grace she moved toward her husband saying, "I'm glad your work is done for now my evening begins."

Abd-al-Rahman put his arm around her but his gaze remained on Alec and Henry. González said jokingly, "You have only one rival, Tabari, and that is Ziyadah."

She pouted coquettishly. "I know," she said sweetly, "and isn't it silly to be jealous of a ghost?"

Henry told Alec, "I want to get out of here."

As they excused themselves, and moved toward the door Abd-al-Rahman said quietly, "I would like my keys, please."

Alec turned quickly, fearful for his horse's safety.

The Sheikh laughed loudly. "Oh, you may keep the one to *his* stall," he said with sarcasm. "It is only the other keys that I need."

When Alec followed Henry from the room he was conscious of Tabari's perfume. He thought of the mares waiting for her in the corner of the field and of her being content only to watch them.

"Have a good night," Abd-al-Rahman called as they shut the door.

Much later Alec stood by his bedroom window. It was partly open and there was a hint of rain in the cold night air.

From somewhere behind him Henry said, "You ought to go to bed."

"Why don't you?"

"I'm waiting for tomorrow."

"So am I," Alec said.

"I'm not closin' my eyes until you do."

"He's got the house bolted front and back. I

191

couldn't get out if I wanted to — which I don't," Alec added hastily.

"Then what're you starin' into the night for?"

"I'm looking at the gardens. They're pretty all lighted up as they are. If he lets us go, we won't be seeing them any more."

"Humph!" snorted Henry.

Alec shrugged his shoulders. Henry needn't be suspicious. What reason would he have for trying to leave this house and trailing Ziyadah? Especially since everybody knew they were leaving tomorrow. It would be too dangerous. If Henry was right, someone was just waiting for a last chance at him and his horse. It was far better and safer to stay indoors.

Turning away from the window, he found Henry standing at the fireplace. Red-and-orange flames licked greedily at the big logs, casting ragged shadows in the semi-darkened room. "Go to bed," Alec repeated. "You're beat."

Henry didn't answer and Alec turned back to the window. He liked the coldness of the night air. He even wished it would rain so he could feel it on his face. Like Henry, he was mixed up and a little scared. They hadn't found what they'd come after but he was glad to be leaving. He stared into the darkness without actually seeing anything.

Were they prisoners in this fortress or would Abd-al-Rahman let them go tomorrow as he'd promised? Only morning would provide the answer, for that was when González was prepared to leave.

Suddenly he felt a horrible net of gloom descend upon him. He tried to shake it off by concentrating on the play of the fountains below. It didn't help. He found himself listening for strange sounds in the night and occasionally he would start at the sudden crackling of wood in the fire. He looked down into the darkness of the courtyard. There was a sheer drop of three high stories, making him feel more than ever like a prisoner.

A long while later he turned away from the window. Henry was asleep in a chair beside the fire. "I'm going to Abd-al-Rahman," he said aloud, as if doing so made it easier for him to leave the room. "I can't let him think of me as a coward. I couldn't live with myself if I did. I want to tell him where Ziyadah went. He can follow the trail himself. I don't want Ziyadah. I've got the Black. All I want is to keep him."

Henry snored in reply.

Leaving the room, Alec walked down the long gallery until he came to Abd-al-Rahman's bedroom. He knocked on the door. There was no answer. For a moment he stood there undecided, then he turned the knob. The door was unlocked and the room empty. A small fire burned in the fireplace, casting its flickering light upon the elaborately carved wardrobe cabinet in the corner of the room. The door to Tabari's adjoining bedroom was open but there was no light or sound from within. Abd-al-Rahman was perhaps still downstairs with his wife and González.

A few minutes later Alec looked into the great living room and saw Tabari and Angel González sitting before the fire. They didn't see him and he closed the door again, deciding to go to the strange, bare room in which he'd found Abd-al-Rahman once before. As he passed through the silent corridors and halls he was aware only of the loud creaking made by his own hurried steps. When he came to the room he sought he knocked softly upon the door.

There was no answer and he entered, surprised at finding the door unlocked and the room empty. A dim light shone from the small desk lamp. Alec decided this must mean that Abd-al-Rahman would return at any moment, so he sat down on one of the hard, straight-backed chairs and waited.

The room was damp and cold. Alec looked at the empty fireplace, recalling vividly the big logs burning everywhere else. The old wire screen was rusty, as was the grate. Evidently there hadn't been a fire there in many years.

Outside he could hear someone locking up the house. He couldn't be mistaken because the great bolts and chains made a lot of noise. A chill ran through him and he rose from the chair, stamping his feet as if to warm them. What was the matter with him anyway?

He recalled how the dust and closeness of this small room had almost stifled him on his first visit. Now he was terribly cold. The night and the dampness accounted for it, he told himself. He reached for a book on the desk and blew the dust from it. It was printed in English so he decided to pass a few minutes reading it.

The book was about the Bedouin and his horse, written by an authority on desert tribes. Most of the history Alec had read before so he skipped lightly over that section. As he went on, he moved the desk lamp closer so he might have more light. He concentrated on the text in front of him: *"The pure Arabian horse has been so intensely inbred through centuries that very often he is not a prolific breeding animal."*

Alec looked up from the book, staring ahead in the dim light from the lamp. Might this not be true of Ziyadah? Was it possible that Abd-al-Rahman wanted the Black because he was

Ziyadah's fastest son and a *proven* sire? Were all the pieces of this crazy jigsaw puzzle falling into place at last?

Alec read further: *"Black Arabians have always been rare and sheikhs want them for their exclusive use if they are fortunate enough to breed one or steal one."*

Ziyadah was a chestnut, according to Tabari, his coat of burnished copper "so highly polished that it reflected the sun's rays," she had said. The Black was coal-black, as black as tar, as black as night itself. Was this another jigsaw piece falling into place? Did Abd-al-Rahman want the Black for himself?

The room seemed much warmer. Or was it only the dim light from the lamp that made him think so? Alec's eyelids felt very heavy and he blinked his eyes in order to stay awake.

Just one more page, he promised himself, then if the Sheikh hadn't returned he'd go. It said here . . . but he'd known . . . he'd known this part all along . . . *"Through their long history Bedouins have treated choice foals like their own children, often taking them into their tents to sleep and making them an integral part of their household. Such a relationship has made the Arabian horse the most intelligent . . ."* Alec's eyes blinked sleepily, *". . . of its race. It will come at call. It will fight in defense of its master. It will . . ."*

The boy's head nodded and his eyes closed. A moment later he was fast asleep.

It was the sound of a rising wind that awakened him. Still half asleep he listened to its lonely wail and then he remembered where he was. How did the wind get into this small closed room? He looked at the narrow stained-glass windows which flanked the fireplace. They were tightly shut. The fireplace. Of course! The huge chimney was filled with the night wind.

He wondered what time it was and how long he'd slept. The open book lay before him and he was about to close it and leave the room when he remembered the strange dream he'd been having.

It was of an old Arab chieftain and his most prized stallion. The horse, like Ziyadah, was a golden chestnut and he slept on a great white fur rug at the foot of the chieftain's bed.

Alec half-smiled at his mental picture of the old man and his horse, and shut the book. Then it occurred to him that his dream might not have been so ridiculous after all. A rich Arab sheikh might easily keep his horse in such luxury, close to him, for fear of his being stolen.

Alec's hand brushed against his nose as he returned the book to its proper place. He stood up. The odor of the liniment he'd used on the Black was in the room. It was faint but his sense of smell was keen and there was no mistake about it. He raised his hands, sniffing them, and smelled only bath soap. Then he sniffed his clothes, thinking he might have spilled some of the liquid on them. No, they were free of the odor. He sat down again, trying to shrug off his interest in the faint odor of the liniment. After all, what difference did it make where it came from or for what reason? It wasn't from the Black, who was locked safely in his stall. Any number of horses might have it on their legs. *But why did he smell it here in this room?*

He remembered what he'd read of the close relationship between the Arab and his horse — and he recalled his dream.

He got to his feet, believing his thoughts to be even more fantastic than his dream had been. And yet . . . Was it the flickering light that accounted for his sudden dizziness? Or was it because of what he was going to do?

He walked across the room slowly and quietly and stopped in front of the huge fireplace. He smelled rust from the screen and grate, the dampness of the stone. Stronger than ever, too, was the odor of the liniment. It seemed to be coming from the chimney. Could it be coming from *below*? But was it so strange to keep a horse hidden in a fortress-like pile of ancient stone such as this? Couldn't it be expected of old Barjas ben Ishak that he would have built secret stalls in his cellars in order to insure the safety of his prized horses? And might not Ziyadah have as much use for the leg liniment as the Black after last night's chase?

19 BLACK DEPTHS

Alec left the room. No noise now, he warned himself. There was only a dim light burning in the long gallery, and when he reached a window from where he could see the lighted stable-yard clock he discovered it was after three o'clock. He'd slept much longer than he'd realized. But it was just as well, he told himself, for there was less chance of waking anyone now.

He went from hall to hall, softly turning knobs and listening for the faintest of sounds. But the house was very still with only an occasional crackle and pop from a dying fire. Despite his stealth, Alec hurried for he intended to cover a lot of ground. He didn't waste any time going upstairs but searched the bottom floor for doors and stairways that would take him to the cellars. He was certain the area below would be immense, for the main floor, reached by the two flights of outside steps, was more than fifty feet above the ground.

Toward the back of the house he found what he was after. Sliding back the bolts of a door off the kitchen, he stopped before a steep stairway. For a moment he hesitated, thinking he could smell danger in the intense blackness of the passageway. But although there was a clammy, musty odor about the place, he could not smell the liniment.

He would not have gone down if he hadn't found the light switch. It meant that kitchen help used these stairs. There was nothing to fear but his own uneasiness. He shut the door before flicking on the switch. The lights were not as bright as he would have liked but he had no trouble finding his way. He sniffed the air constantly for the sharp, familiar odor of the liniment but smelled only the clamminess of old earth.

When he came to the bottom of the steps he stopped, his eyes moving slowly over cases of stored furniture.

After all, this was just another ancient home in the mountains, he told himself reassuringly. There were many of them in Europe, just as old and just as big. He listened to a distant hum. It was only a dynamo, supplying electricity. There was the sound of a pump, too, hoisting water five stories high and probably to the stables as well.

Then why did he start at the slightest noise? *Was it because he felt he was being watched?* But that, too, was silly. There was no one down here but himself.

The cellar was a maze of intricate passageways where anyone could have been hidden. On either side of the long corridors were barrel-shaped vaults which in their day could have been used to stable horses but now held old furniture and pictures, stoves and fixtures of all kinds including bathtubs and kitchen sinks. There was nothing to get excited about at all, nothing to fear.

Alec walked up and down the wide corridors, knowing he had found what he'd sought, the emergency stables which Barjas ben Ishak had built so many centuries ago. But they held no horses now, only unused furniture and appliances.

He stopped before one of the round, massive pillars that supported the cellar roof. Was the unused fireplace in the small, bare room directly above this? It might be. The great pillar probably helped support the chimney as well as the cellar roof. But he still smelled only clamminess in the cellars. Where had the odor of liniment come from? Outside?

Returning to the main floor, he bolted the cellar door again and stole softly down the hall. There was no sound of anyone moving through the big house, and he no longer felt, as he had below, that someone was watching him. He wanted to find out if the bottle of liniment was in the tack room where he had left it. Also, he could make certain the Black was safe. But even if he had had the key to the front door he couldn't have slipped the heavy bolts without awakening the household.

From outside came the rumble of thunder. From a window Alec could see that the sky was heavily clouded, the full moon emerging occasionally to spread a milky-white glow over the darkened gardens. It was now close to four o'clock by the stableyard clock and dawn would be breaking before very long. If he planned to search further, he decided, he'd better do it now under the cover of darkness.

He opened the window and, leaning out, saw that there was a ledge under the window that went all the way to a corner of the house (where he knew the kitchen area to be), and beyond it.

It was wide enough for a good foothold. He wouldn't have any trouble reaching the corner and from there he'd be able to drop into the stream. He'd made dives from such a height plenty of times. But why do it? Why even get wet? What had he to gain if he found the bottle of leg liniment missing from the tack room? What would it prove? Only that someone else was using it. But where? And was the Black safe in his stall?

He raised the window higher. His hands groped along the outer wall until he'd found a good hold, then he pulled himself onto the ledge and began inching toward his objective.

If, as he believed, Ziyadah was stabled *here* and not running free in the mountains, another piece in this whole crazy jigsaw fell into place. But who tended Ziyadah? Who opened and closed the big gate, sending him into the mountains?

And what about Angel González and María? What part did they play in this? Had they really returned to make certain he and Henry were all right? Or were they in some way connected with last night's appearance of Ziyadah?

The moon came out and Alec stopped moving, afraid that he might be seen in its light. Somewhere a dog barked. Alec could hear the splashing of the fountains below.

There was only one question he needed to have answered: If Ziyadah was here, where was he stabled? If not in the cellars, could he be somewhere in the barns themselves?

A heavy cloud shrouded the moon and Alec went on. Reaching the corner of the building, he looked down. He knew that the water below was dark and deep, but this was no time to hesitate or turn back. He sat down on the ledge, pushed himself clear of the building, and dropped.

A moment later he pulled himself out of the stream, having learned abruptly that the water was extremely cold in addition to being deep. He favored his right ankle, which he had twisted upon hitting the water. The injury wasn't serious but it slowed him down.

Shivering, he skirted the stableyard and climbed the knoll to the stallion barn. To add to his discomfort it started to rain. As he bent his head into the dark and streaming downpour, he slipped on the wet grass, hurting his ankle even more.

The Black heard him and snorted. "Go back to sleep, black horse," Alec said outside the closed door. "I'm the only one who would have picked such a night to go swimming. But I'm glad you're safe. I was worried."

His teeth chattering, Alec went to the cabinet in the tack room where he had left the liniment. The bottle was there, just where he had put it, and the level was the same. He took it down and then, still feeling cold and miserable, went into the stall that had once belonged to Ziyadah. He sat down in the deep, clean straw.

"You dream too much," he told himself. "Worse still, you let your imagination run wild. There is no Ziyadah hidden here. He runs free in the mountains. You chased him yourself, so you should know. Tomorrow you'll pay for all this, for you can't get back in the house without waking everybody up."

The rain whirling outside seemed to make his head spin, and it occurred to him that perhaps he had hurt his ankle even more than he had thought. Taking off his shoe and sock, he rubbed on some of the liniment in the belief that what had helped the Black's leg would help his. His eyes and nose smarted from the strong fumes, and he was reminded again of the cellar stables.

Now if he had been old Barjas ben Ishak and had been building this place, what provision would he have made for his most prized stallion in case of an unexpected raid?

Alec had no ready answer to this question. And just then the rain stopped as abruptly as it had begun. The moon came out briefly and the dogs began barking again. In the fields the crickets chirred and the wind howled. The liniment felt good on Alec's bare foot. He shoved it into the straw and covered it completely for added warmth and comfort. Then he took off his other wet shoe and sock and stuck that foot into the straw too, wishing he could remove his wet clothes as well. Why not, if he got old Nazar's blanket from the chair outside? He started to get up, his bare feet pressing deep into the bottom of the straw. Cold metal brushed against his right foot and, thinking it something that had been dropped there, he bent down to pick it up. But he couldn't budge it. Leaning over for a closer look, he discovered that it was a large ring, made of gold and fastened to the floor. He pulled it again, wondering why it was there.

Suddenly a soft hum filled the stall, as if some mechanism had started. Then with a faint grinding of gears the straw floor dropped, taking Alec down slowly. The last thing he saw as he descended was the ghostly light of the moon coming through the stall door.

20 BLACK WORLD

The long drop and the darkness all around gave
Alec the feeling he had been descending for an
eternity. The faint hum seemed to have become
a hideous roar of grinding, chattering iron teeth
and wheels. Slowly, heavily, the lift went
down, down . . . and if Alec had had a chance
to do it over again he never would have touched
the gold ring without first having gone for
Henry.

Suddenly a dim light penetrated the darkness, and only then did Alec realize that the lift
mechanism wasn't making as much noise as he
had thought. Instead, it was turning smoothly,
almost softly, and he could smell the heavy oil

that lubricated it. Finally the vibrations ceased altogether and the lift came to a stop.

Alec saw a small, bare bulb burning on a rocky wall outside the lift. There was a narrow opening in the wall and the air coming from it was clammy. The opening led to a passageway, and Alec had no doubt that many horses had passed through it.

The way was pitch-dark and he had no desire to travel it without a light. Yet he stepped from the straw floor into the opening and stared into the blackness. It was as silent as a grave. Turning back, he noticed for the first time that there were two switches set in the wall next to the electric light bulb. One or the other must operate the lift. He pulled the top one. But instead of the whir of a motor, there was a sudden lighting of bare bulbs every thirty feet or so along the passageway. Quickly Alec turned the lights off, afraid that already he had warned someone of his presence. For many minutes he listened but there were no footsteps on the stone, no sound of any breathing but his own.

When he was certain no one was coming, he pulled the lower switch. The faint hum of a working mechanism started again and the straw floor began to rise. He stopped it, even though common sense told him to take it to the surface at once and let Henry know what he had discovered.

He stared into the dark passageway, breathing the air that smelled of old earth and stone. Carried on the damp air too was the odor of liniment . . . and it was not from the liniment on his ankle. Slowly, ever so slowly, he made up his mind, listening only to a reckless inner voice that told him to find out what lay at the end of the tunnel. He threw the switch that lit the passageway and went forward quickly, his bare feet making no noise on the stone floor.

He walked beneath the dim white lights, finding it far more difficult to accept this tunnel-like passage than the lift that had brought him down. Such raising and lowering mechanisms had been in use long before the time of Barjas ben Ishak. In fact, the Romans had used such lifts, cranked by men, to raise wild animals to the arena from underground pens! But here in the bowels of the rock, the ancient stone floor of the tunnel was smooth beneath his feet, and on the walls were sculptured figures of horses. Alec had no doubt that this underground shaft had been hand-hewn by many hundreds of men over a long period of time. It was no work of nature. For further proof he had only to look at the arched roof and the cylindrical borings that ran upwards for ventilation.

The strong odor of liniment floated toward him, carried from the distant regions of the tunnel. He hurried along, sometimes breaking into a half-run as one might do when going home late on a semi-lighted street and feeling very much alone. Finally he came to a heavy wooden door. It was wide open!

But if the open door was inviting the darkness beyond was not. Alec looked in but could see nothing. He had gone far enough, he told himself. He should go back and get Henry.

But might not Ziyadah's stall be on the other side? Or had Abd-al-Rahman's quest of the golden stallion been just a ruse to acquire the Black?

Alec turned away from the door, his thoughts in a turmoil. Then he saw a switch on the wall. If he pulled it, would it light the room on the other side of the doorway? Would he see Ziyadah, *the sire of the Black?* He could feel his heart pounding like a hammer. He pulled the switch.

The lights in the tunnel went out and he stood motionless in complete darkness. He could easily have thrown the switch back on again but he didn't. Instead he waited for his eyes to become accustomed to the lack of light. After a few minutes he was able to detect a faint glow on the other side of the door. The skin on his throat tightened as, contrary to his better judgment, he slipped through the doorway.

It was not a room which he had entered but a long and wide corridor, at the end of which burned the remains of a dying fire. This was the glow he had seen. He went toward it slowly, one step at a time, feeling his way cautiously. Unlike the passage he had just left, the walls here were of smooth mortar. He believed that he was somewhere beneath the cellars he had searched only a short while ago. Barjas ben Ishak, it was clear, had not been content with his cellar stables any more than he had been with those outside the house. So he had built these secret chambers to which he could take his most highly prized stallions whenever danger threatened.

Alec had taken thirty-one steps down the corridor, counting as he went along. Then his hand touched wood instead of stone. He stopped and ran his fingers over the surface. It was a paneled door, probably made of oak. Suddenly Alec froze. There was a horse on the other side of the door!

The odor of leg liniment was very strong, and Alec had heard the horse start up in the straw, rustling it and coming over to the door. Alec touched an iron bolt and there was a welcome nicker on the other side. How he wished he had a light so he could see what he was doing! He ran his fingers over the bolt, searching for a switch. Then he went on in the darkness until he came to the stone wall again. After some groping, he found the protruding switch and pulled it.

A light went on in the stall but not in the corridor. It shone through high iron bars that rose from the top of the wooden door to the ceiling. Alec pulled himself up onto the bars and looked inside.

Standing beneath a protected light bulb was a stallion who could be no other than *Ziyadah*! He was as still as finely polished marble, his eyes on the door. Then he heard the sharp intake of Alec's breath and, turning swiftly, jumped to the side of his stall.

Ziyadah's eyes, widely set apart like the Black's, were a light brown, almost as golden as his coat. They glowed, and when he rolled them, crescents of white eyeball showed for an instant. He snorted at Alec, his nostrils flaring. There was no doubt he had been expecting someone else.

He jumped again, angrily tossing his small head. His hoofs barely touched the straw as he leaped from one side of the stall to the other. At the moment it was not hard for Alec to believe that the horse the natives called "Firetail" could literally walk the sky.

Finally the stallion swept over to the far corner of his big stall.

"Whoever you're for, you're for him alone," Alec said. "Is it Abd-al-Rahman?"

Ziyadah pranced up and down, and in the shadows his hoofs glowed, sending a thousand shafts of light about the stall. Alec gasped. So this was the answer to the constant rain of sparks that came from his flying hoofs! There was nothing ghostly about them. *His hoofs were encased in rubber sheaths which were covered with sequins of many colors!* They sparkled brilliantly in the play of light. They would also leave no tracks.

Who was responsible for this sham?

Alec looked down the darkened corridor. The fire still burned faintly. If he made no noise . . . if he was very, very careful, he might find out . . . providing the person he was seeking was there by the fire and asleep.

He lowered himself to the stone floor and turned off the stall light. He took one step forward and then another. He had come too far to turn back, to go for Henry. Now that he was so close to finding the answer to his question, nothing could have stopped him from going on.

As he got closer to the fire he was able to see

his way more clearly. There were several corridors running off from the big one, and they were similar to those in the cellars above. Here, too, were the same vault-like rooms which could have been used as stables generations ago. There were also the massive pillars to support the ceiling and the borings for ventilation. The chimneys, too, supplied this subcellar with air. It was from the chimney down here that the smell of liniment on Ziyadah's legs had reached him. He was certain of it. He was now in a room several stories directly below the small, bare room he had left hours ago.

The fire popped, flinging out a glowing ember upon the stone floor. Feeble as it was it added to the room's illumination. Alec strained his eyes searching the darkness. *The room was empty.* Softly he went to the fire and put on another log.

The dry wood caught quickly, its flickering gleams brightening the place. There was a large low couch directly opposite the fireplace, complete with tanned skins for blankets and a large pillow. It was apparent that somebody slept here. *But who?*

There were a few black carpets scattered about the worn stone floor, and while right now the room was cold and dark, it had an atmosphere of having been lived in for many generations. The dark wood furniture was ancient and highly polished. There were several tall, straight-backed chairs and a huge desk and lamp. At the far end of the room was a small alcove containing a modern cooking range, a sink, and cabinets stocked with food. Just off the kitchenette was a bathroom and shower.

Alec returned to the main room. Here, as elsewhere, the sculptured figures of horses stood out from the walls. They were worn smooth with age as was this room. Yet somebody had equipped it with modern appliances and was living here! *Who*?

He went to the desk, running his hand over the smooth dark wood. No dust. This was the desk of a person who occupied it often.

Alec tried the drawers. They were all locked but one. In it he found plain white paper and envelopes, pens and ink. He was about to close the drawer when he saw the snapshot that was caught in a back corner. Withdrawing it carefully so as not to tear it, he held it up and studied it. The picture showed Abu Ishak, Tabari's father, holding the Black. It must have been taken shortly before his death, Alec decided. He studied the snapshot for a long time. Abu Ishak had been a very good and close friend in the short time they'd known each other. Without him there would have been no Ziyadah, no

Black, no continuation at all of the breeding program begun so many years ago.

Alec closed the desk drawer, his mind full of questions. If he had been able to open the other drawers would he have found charts and pedigrees in Abu Ishak's handwriting? Who used this desk? Who had the key?

The fire brightened, throwing its gleams farther into the room. It was a strange place and a lonely one. Suddenly Alec noticed that the far wall was draped with a large black curtain or tapestry. He froze momentarily. Was there still another room? Could someone be hiding there? He listened, and then, having heard nothing, stepped forward slowly, his bare feet making no noise on the black carpets. The covering, when he reached it, proved to be a curtain. Carefully Alec pulled it aside. A brilliant galaxy of blue, red and orange sparks burst in his face.

He dropped to the stone floor, dodging the blow he thought would surely follow. There was no sound except for the crackling of the fire. The black curtain hung motionlessly. For several minutes Alec lay on the floor, waiting for almost anything to happen.

The sparks had been no different from Ziyadah's streaming trail. Were they, like the stallion's sequined hoofs, only a trick? If so what had he to fear from them?

Alec rose to his feet and drew aside the curtain again. The light from the fire penetrated the alcove that was there, playing upon a long tassel-like cape that was covered with large, glittering sequins. Alec removed it from its hook. Attached to it was a light harness that could be fastened to a horse's tail, securing the long cape while at the same time allowing it to whip behind in the wind. . . . *Of course! Firetail! Ziyadah!*

Alec's eyes swept the alcove and what he saw then was even more astounding than the sequined cape. There on a rack was a light racing saddle of golden leather! Hanging beside it was a racing bridle of the same lightness and color!

For the first time Alec asked himself, "Could Ziyadah have been ridden last night — and all the other nights before? Had the golden stallion not run alone?" The answer came easily now. He had carried a rider to guide him on his way, to open and close the big gate! Of course, of course, of course!

All the parts of the puzzle had fallen together, all save one . . . *who was the rider?* From a box on a small shelf Alec picked up a flashlight with a red lens. Here too was the eerie light that had seemed to float in the air, up and down the mountainsides, whenever the ghost horse had appeared. Put a rider on Ziyadah's back carrying this flashlight, using it at will, and, like the sequins which reflected the moonlight, there was nothing ghostly about the whole thing at all. No more ghostly than the plastic hoof which lay beside the flashlight . . . a hoof which could make the kind of print Alec had seen before, very stubby and deep. It too was no more ghostly than the bottle of liniment on the same shelf.

Alec was no longer afraid. Reasonable, sensible explanations to what he had seen in the night encouraged him to go on in his search for the person responsible for this whole fantastic plot. Who was the rider? Where was he hiding? Alec walked in the direction of Ziyadah's stall until he came to the first corridor opening off the big one. He turned down it, shortly coming to a pair of tall double doors which he opened, carefully, but without hesitation. He found himself looking into what seemed to be a great darkened pit or void. There was a wall switch on his right and it clicked faintly beneath his touch as the lights went on.

The first thing Alec noticed were the plaques on the insides of the doors. The gold figures were of the boy and the rearing horse. Beyond was an enormous arena with a tanbark floor and row after row of jumps of different kinds and heights . . . jumps over brush and banks, stones and timber and water. It was a schooling arena with every kind of obstacle and barrier that could conceivably arise in front of a horse!

The jumps were new but the arena wasn't. It was about the size of a bull ring, but more oblong than circular. At one end was a long flight of stone steps leading to a door. As Alec walked across the tanbark he found himself thinking of the men and horses who must have occupied this impressive arena so many generations ago.

He stopped at the foot of the staircase. Without a doubt it led to the main house and someone's room. Prepared but tense, he mounted the stairs.

At the top the knob turned noiselessly beneath his hand and he opened the door, at the same time turning off the lights in the arena from a switch near the door. The arena should be dark, just as he had found it. He stood in the blackness of the doorway and the seconds ticked by with nothing happening. Could he smell danger beyond? Or was it just his imagination playing tricks again?

The passageway was airless and stuffy, unlike any of the others through which he had passed. Then he discovered that he had come to an enclosed circular staircase. He began climbing it in the dark, one step at a time. Round and round and higher and higher he climbed. Could this tower-like staircase be taking him through one of the great conical drums he had seen in the cellars? He kept climbing and circling, stopping occasionally to relieve his dizziness.

At last he came to a wooden door. It had no knob but there was a small hole for his fingers. No noise now, not a careless move, not the faintest sound, Alec told himself. Softly, ever so softly, he slid the door open.

It was pitch-dark within. The air was closer than ever. He sniffed, smelling fabrics even before his hands, reaching out, touched the soft materials.

Curtains? No. But the heavy fabrics accounted for the stifling quality of the room. But was it a room? Might it not be . . . He thrust his hands forward again, still groping but more eager. He felt another piece of fabric, then another and another. They hung on wooden hangers, one after the other. *Clothes!* He was in a deep bedroom closet! *Whose?*

Straining his ears, he listened. Not a sound. Soon he would find the closet door. But he must be more careful than ever. Who slept in the bedroom beyond?

Suddenly he heard the soft falling back of a

door latch. He ducked down with the sound, slipping into a mass of soft cashmere which must have been an overcoat. He pulled it around him and held his breath. *The very person he sought was entering the closet!*

Alec heard the quick footfalls as the door opened. From his position down on the floor he could see slim legs encased in tight leather the color of gold. Before the door closed he made out the faint glow of a dying fire in the room beyond.

The clothes a few feet from him moved slightly as if a ghost had glided past. Alec raised his eyes, straining them in an attempt to pierce the blackness, but he saw nothing. There was the sound of quick steps, and then the opening and closing of the door to the circular staircase.

Alec rose to his feet, took a step forward as if to follow, then turned back. He went to the door opening into the bedroom and looked inside. The firelight was feeble but it showed him plainly where he was.

The big closet occupied the corner of the bedroom. The floor in front of it was covered with the tanned skin of a mountain lion. The door to the adjoining bedroom was closed and on the bureau was Abd-al-Rahman's large brass key ring.

Alec made up his mind what to do. He slipped out of the closet and past the closed door leading to Tabari's bedroom. His next move would be to get Henry and tell him what he had found. Together they'd face Abd-al-Rahman! But not until it got light and there were others around to hear. Alec glanced back at the closet. He would have liked to have known what the Sheikh was up to but he did not feel equal to meeting Abd-al-Rahman in the darkness below.

The fire popped and Alec jumped. He chided himself for his uneasiness. All he had to do now was to get to the hall door. Only Homsi, who slept in the alcove near the door, presented any problem.

The fire popped again but this time Alec did not jump. He was too absorbed in something else. *For there, sleeping heavily on the bed, was Abd-al-Rahman!*

For many minutes Alec stood absolutely still, his eyes on the bed without seeing it, his face a frozen mask. Finally he turned toward the closet.

Could it be? he asked himself. *Could it?*

The fixed stare left his eyes. Swiftly he ran to the closet, and then started down the circular staircase. From below came the sound of quick footsteps dying away.

Small, bare bulbs lit the way for him. Alec made no attempt to conceal the sound of his own running feet. No longer was there any reason for quiet and secrecy. Now he was certain whom he was chasing. The final piece of the jigsaw puzzle had fallen into place.

21 BLACK DEATH

The arena was empty when Alec reached it. He ran across the tanbark, grateful for the fresher air. Reaching the tall double doors, he pulled them open and didn't bother closing them behind him. The corridor was lighted and he ran the length of it, coming to a stop only when he had to decide whether to turn to Ziyadah's stall or the chamber. He chose the latter and went forward slowly. The room was as he had left it. There was nobody here unless ... Staying close to the wall, Alec slid toward the black-curtained alcove and parted the drapery, alert for any blow that might fall. The tail harness with its long cape of glittering sequins hung on the same peg as before. The racing bridle and saddle were there. So were the red flashlight and the plastic hoof, even the bottle of liniment.

There was only one other place to go. He left the chamber at a run and headed for Ziyadah's stall. The door was closed but the light was on. Alec pulled himself up onto the bars and looked inside. There was no golden stallion standing beneath the overhead light. *Ziyadah was off!*

Alec listened for the sound of hoofs as he ran along the passageway, but he heard nothing. Arriving at the lift, he found it waiting for him. For the first time he hesitated. It was too inviting. His having left the lift below had, of course, given his presence away if nothing else had. The lift had taken Ziyadah to the surface and then been sent down again for him. Why? Perhaps he was more the *hunted* than the hunter!

Alec pulled the wall switch and stepped onto the straw-covered floor of the lift. The faint hum began and the lift rose slowly. Alec put a hand in his pants' pocket for the key to the Black's stall. He had no doubt that Ziyadah and his rider would be waiting for them to follow. This was part of the deadly game being played. He felt confident of the outcome of such a race if it took place on the plain. He believed the Black was more than a match for his sire, while he himself could take care of Ziyadah's rider.

Reaching the surface, he ran over to the barn

doors. They were wide open, and beyond them, in the rain and darkness, he could see Ziyadah's sequin-sheathed hoofs. The stallion was no more than a hundred yards from the barn — and there was a rider on his back.

They were waiting just as he had figured.

The wind blew and the rain was cold. Alec's teeth chattered as he opened the door to the Black's stall. "You're poles apart in size," he told his horse, "but you have a race on your hands. Catch him quick. If he gets to the mountains, he's won, because we won't go on."

The Black wasn't listening. He had seen Ziyadah and his eyes were rolling. His hoofs beat an uneasy cadence in the straw. He whistled and Ziyadah answered.

"He knows you're going after him," Alec said, taking the Black outside. The wind hummed about his ears as he pulled himself up on the stallion's broad back. Pounding hoofs shattered the stillness. Ziyadah was away and running!

The Black bolted after him and Alec sat down to ride as he never had ridden before. He noted Ziyadah's smooth, wavy motion and couldn't help thinking of him again as a ghost horse. The rain dripped from his face onto the Black's sodden mane. Ruefully the thought occurred to him that there couldn't have been a worse time for so fantastic a race. Both horses were in a dead run. The barns dropped quickly behind them and Ziyadah soared over his first jump, a stone fence.

The Black followed, with Alec letting his horse decide for himself when to take off. Arrogantly the Black sprang into the air, folding his hocks under his quarters while he stretched out his forelegs ready for landing. He came down with no break in stride and set out for Ziyadah over the cold, wind-swept fields.

From the drenched ground came a steady plop as the hard running hoofs came down on it. A mist swirled upward, almost concealing the stallions' bodies. Alec watched Ziyadah sweep through it and became uneasy. They were not overtaking the flying horse. He was tackling the stone walls as if they weren't even there! It called for both courage and speed to keep up with him.

The Black would have preferred firm footing to the soft going, but he answered Ziyadah's challenge. He jumped another stone fence right on Ziyadah's heels but lost ground to him when the golden stallion swerved abruptly. Alec, swinging after him in a lightning-swift turn, could hardly see Ziyadah in the ground mist, for he had gained many lengths.

More from habit than need Alec guided his horse. With tremendous strides the Black closed ground. Another stone fence rose before them and with a magnificent leap the Black cleared it. He had no sooner landed than he rose again. This time it was a double fence and he just made it, his hind hoofs clicking against the stone.

Now Alec could make out the outline of the rider on Ziyadah's back. The crouched figure seemed constantly to be looking backward. Then suddenly horse and rider were lost in the deep shadows of the mountain. Alec slowed the Black, wary of what he could not see.

A high timber fence rose before them and the Black stopped abruptly, throwing Alec into his wind-tangled mane. A moment later Alec knocked down the top bars and took his horse over the fence. Ziyadah was nowhere to be seen.

They were only a short distance from the main gate and Alec found it open. Evidently Ziyadah's rider didn't plan to lose him! Alec was sure of this when, a few minutes later, Ziyadah could be seen in the swirling mist less than a hundred yards away. As soon as the Black saw him he was on his way, picking up more and more speed.

Ziyadah cut across the plain where the ditches were deepest. He came upon them at full gallop, sliding down with little loss of stride. The Black followed, but Alec did not push him and Ziyadah drew away.

When they reached the cover of the mountain, Ziyadah had momentarily disappeared. Alec knew where he had gone, for this was where they had left him last night. He walked the Black to the base of the mountain. Ziyadah was up there, waiting for them. Alec hesitated, his eyes on the horse and rider who were no more than fifty feet above them on a narrow, rocky trail. "Come on," he said into the Black's ears. "I've changed my mind."

Dismounting, he led his horse up the trail. It sloped into the wall of the mountain itself, which was the reason so little of it could be seen from below. It widened as they climbed, and a jagged mass of black rock rose on either side.

Up and up they went, finally emerging from the folds of the mountain to follow a great precipice which jutted out over the plain below. For a moment, Alec thought they had come to the end of the trail and would be cast into midair if they went any farther. But the rocky path wound its way around the end of the precipice and folded once more into the wall of the mountain. Ziyadah was nowhere to be seen.

Alec welcomed the black rock that closed in upon them again. He had no stomach for great heights. The trail grew narrower and narrower.

The wind blew in great gusts but the rain had stopped. Also, the first light of dawn had come, enabling Alec to see more of the trail. There was still no sign of Ziyadah, but he had to be just ahead.

"Careful now," Alec warned himself. "It could happen any minute. Watch yourself."

There was no sound of hoofs, not even the Black's. All sound was silenced by the wind from the upper reaches, shrieking past and wailing until the very rock seemed to vibrate.

Suddenly the trail widened and Alec walked faster, his hand on the Black's halter, until he came to a deep cleft in the wall. It seemed to be a natural cave even though the floor was smooth. Alec peered into it. He neither saw nor heard anything, yet the Black's head was raised high, indicating he had caught a scent. Alec knew it must be Ziyadah. Yet the Black did not snort or whistle. For reasons known only to himself, Alec's horse was quiet even though he had winded another stallion.

Alec waited for the gray light of dawn to brighten, warming his chilled body by pulling the Black close to him. There was no movement to the stallion's head or eyes; he continued staring into the cavern. The rocky walls above changed in color from gray to pink, and the morning light finally reached the trail, allowing Alec to see more of the cavern. A pale light shone deep within and he knew there was an opening on the other side!

Deciding that it was light enough for him to make his way, Alec led the Black into the cavern. With every stride the stallion's eagerness mounted until Alec knew his blasting whistle was about to fill the air. But before it came, the stillness was shattered by the sound of a shot. The bullet whizzed close to the Black's head!

Alec jerked his horse against the wall as the sound of the shot echoed through the cave. No other shots followed. But all at once Ziyadah was running through the opening at the opposite end of the cavern!

Alec let out a wild yell of fury before he mounted the Black, and with shoulders bent low over the stallion's neck, shouted, "Let's go!"

The Black swept through the cavern and out onto a narrow canyon trail, drawing closer and closer to the flying horse.

Ziyadah knew his way well, finding the smoothest part of the canyon floor and running with swift, fierce strides. The Black, following him, had his head stretched out, his teeth bared.

Alec's blood ran hot with rage. He had no control over the violence which flowed between himself and his mount. He sought revenge with all his heart and soul. Never before in his life had he felt this way. His one objective was to ride down the person on Ziyadah's back who had sought to destroy his horse.

Run, Black, run!

As the Black jumped over the snags and stones in his path, Alec had trouble keeping his seat. Never had he had less control over the Black! He realized that the maddened horse was racing to kill and that there might be nothing he could do to stop him. Down steep gorges and ravines the Black followed Ziyadah, holding his long swift strides without a break. Closer and closer drew the pursuing stallion, his whistle repeating his constant challenge.

There was a slight break in Ziyadah's smooth strides as he approached a row of low-growing bushes. He jumped, clearing the thicket easily, but his long tail caught in the thorns, and this seemed to startle him. He landed hard and his first strides were short and jerky. He regained his smoothness but only for a moment; then he faltered again, and this time he stumbled.

The Black had leaped over the thicket as if it hadn't been there, bearing down upon Ziyadah with thunder rolling from his hoofs.

Alec knew he had to be careful in pulling the Black away from Ziyadah. A mistake at this speed meant certain death. His wind-blurred eyes made it difficult to gauge distances. Ziyadah was swiftly falling back. He was breaking! He swerved but the black stallion followed with a nimble, tremendous bound and reached out for him.

The rider on Ziyadah's back turned and lifted

a black-handled gun. Alec saw nothing but the barrel being leveled at his horse. He gripped with his knees and reached for the gun as the rider screamed, *"Death to Shêtân! Death, death, death."* There was a horrible impact of running bodies before the gun could be fired, followed by a sickening stop as the horses rose as one, twisting upon each other and fighting in the air!

Alec saw the curve of his horse's black mane coming back at him, then he became tangled with the rider on Ziyadah! One hand clawed at his face while the other waved the gun. It went off with a short, yellow burst of flame and a roar. Ziyadah screamed and the Black fell back. Alec tumbled to the ground, striking his head, and was enveloped in darkness. . . .

22 BLACK CURTAIN

"... It is ironical — is it not? — that my father should bequeath to you the devil responsible for his death?
But for that, we would have destroyed him. ..."

Alec well remembered her letter. He had received it long ago and only last night he had recalled it, there in Abd-al-Rahman's room where the scent of Tabari's perfume clung after she had passed him. Now the subtle but heady odor was strong in his nostrils.

He didn't want to move or open his eyes. Not just yet. His skin tingled with the faster beat of his heart. What had happened to the Black?

There was no sound, nothing but the smell of Tabari's perfume. Then . . . then he heard it, a soft slippered foot coming closer. He waited another moment, gathering himself.

Now!

He rolled his body, striking out and toppling Tabari to the ground. Her pale eyes, staring up at him, blazed with wrath and fury. She screamed at him and tried to loosen his hold upon her shoulders.

Alec stared in fascinated horror at the change in her, holding her down even more firmly as she sought to bite him. Through blurred eyes he looked at her, wanting to know what had happened to his horse. She turned her head away.

His eyes followed hers. There were no horses to be seen in this part of the canyon. Alec shook her hard. "What have you done?" he shouted, recalling the short, yellow spurt of flame from the gun. His anger drained quickly from him. If the Black was dead . . .

"Let me go!" she screamed, trying to kick her way free. But he would not give way until he knew what had happened to his horse.

His hard hands tightened about her shoulders. "You had no right!" he said wildly.

"No right?" she screamed back in his face. "No right, when he killed my father? For years

I have planned this day! I swore revenge upon my father's grave!"

Alec simply stared at her, unable to believe that an accident had turned this girl into a hate-filled woman. There was nothing youthful about her now. Her beauty had shrunken into ugliness. Her features quivered with her deep loathing as she said bitterly, "But for him my father would be alive. And for that he, too, is dead!"

Alec pinned her clenched fists to her sides. "You're sure?" he asked crazily.

"How could I have missed?" she asked, trying to pull away. But her voice had the uncertainty of a child who might have failed in something and couldn't understand how it had come about. "However, my Ziyadah will finish him if I did not."

"I wouldn't be so certain," Alec said evenly. Ziyadah could not defeat his horse in a fair fight. He saw the gun lying a few feet away. There was no need to do anything about it. Tabari would not get a chance to use it again, and he had no desire even to pick it up.

"If you let me go we can find them," she said quietly, as if inviting him to one of her afternoon teas.

"First," he said, "tell me why."

"I told you, I swore revenge upon my father's

grave!" Once again her voice was vicious yet she paused, her eyes laughing in her ridicule of him. "Don't look so shocked, my young Alec. You know the ways of my people too well. *A life for a life, remember?*"

"But this is an animal. Your father would be ashamed," Alec said bitterly.

"Perhaps," she replied without anger, "but I do not think so. You see, it was he who provided me with the means to carry out my revenge."

"The means," Alec repeated bewilderedly. She looked like a little girl again, sincere in her defiance but at the same time insecure. "How?" he asked.

"By leaving a letter telling me that Ziyadah was alive and stabled here under the care of old Nazar."

Alec waited for this to sink in. "Then Ziyadah hadn't been lost after all?"

"Of course not. The story of his loss and death was a ruse to outwit my father's enemies. He was afraid of Ziyadah being stolen."

"By the same enemies who stole the Black later?"

She nodded her head, attempting once more to get up.

Alec let go of her and she jumped to her feet. "Had you never recovered him my father would be alive. Do you understand?" She spoke almost in a hiss.

Alec shivered as he stared at her, trying to understand. Finally he said, "Because I did recover him I too was included in your revenge. Is that it?"

"No, I used *you* to reach him," she said quietly and without feeling as she turned and stalked away. "I watched you tonight until you left the house. I knew you'd follow if Ziyadah appeared, but I didn't expect you to find his stall or me. You are too lucky, Alec Ramsay."

Alec walked beside her in the gray dawn. "Does your husband know about you and Ziyadah?"

"Of course not. He would be — " She stopped as if only then realizing that she could no longer keep her secret from Abd-al-Rahman. "I suppose you will tell him?" Suddenly she became agitated and trembling as she looked Alec straight in the eyes. "He will be displeased. Would you . . . would you in the memory of my father . . . ?"

"No," Alec said, unable to understand her girlish pleading after all the terrible things she had done. "The horse your father gave me may be dead," he said bitterly. "Isn't that enough reason for my telling your husband of your deceit? You didn't train Ziyadah overnight, Tabari. How long did you come here before you rode your 'ghost' horse through the mountains and news of him reached your husband?"

Tabari was still trembling from head to foot and Alec almost felt sorry for her. "I came often," she said, "usually when he thought I had gone to London." Her face was pale. "Please..."

"No," Alec repeated. But he said it with compassion, remembering again the girl of the desert he had known so well. He remembered her laughter as she had ridden beside him, trying to send her Jôhar past the Black. He remembered many other things. Then why couldn't he understand the shock her father's death had been to her? No — not when it drove her to take such brutal revenge upon a horse. But then, he reminded himself, he was not of Arab blood. There were many laws of the desert people which he would never understand.

"Tell your husband the truth," he said finally. "If anyone forgives you it should be he. I never will."

"*Forgive me!*" she exclaimed, suddenly vindictive again. "For what? For revenging the death of my father? You are a fool! I want no one's forgiveness, not even my husband's!"

Alec wasn't looking at her or listening to her.

Down the canyon he could see a dusky silhouette against the morning's grayness.

His horse was alive!

"There will be more than that for your husband to forgive," Alec told Tabari.

She was staring at him. "More?" she asked. "How could there be more?" Her puzzled eyes searched his. Finally she found her answer. *"Ziyadah dead?* You're being ridiculous, Alec Ramsay." She laughed but stopped abruptly, and her eyes, following his, became wild and desperate like an animal's at bay. A scream burst from her and she ran forward.

Alec sought to catch her arm but she wrenched herself free. He felt only deep grief for her as, with tears in his eyes, he followed her into a blurred world which held only his horse. The Black was motionless and without sound. Ziyadah lay on the ground a few feet away. The Black had not shrilled his clarion call of victory because he had not killed the other stallion. There were no marks of his hoofs or teeth on Ziyadah. There was only a bullet hole, high on the golden neck.

Great sobs racked the girl's body as she stooped to kneel beside her horse. And only then did Alec realize how much she had loved Ziyadah. For the first time in a long while he understood her, for he would have reacted in the same way if it had been the Black who was down. Her own gun had killed her horse and no one could change things now. Ziyadah was dead.

When Alec put his hand on her arm she made no attempt to break free. For a long while she gave vent to dreadful, heartrending sobs. Finally they died away, and nothing but the shell was left of the spiteful woman who had plotted the Black's death with such cold calculation. Now she was like a very small girl, afraid to run away, afraid to go home. She flung herself upon the ground.

The Black came to them and Alec put a hand on his wet neck. "I guess we're going to keep a lot to ourselves," he told his horse. "We're going to forget there ever was a Ziyadah and that we caught up with him too late. We're going to let Tabari tell her husband as much or as little as she pleases. It's enough that we're going home *together*."

He lifted the girl to her feet. "Come on," he said, "please."

She nodded listlessly, her eyes swollen from weeping. "But I don't like to leave him alone," she said.

"You can come back," he answered, "with your husband. You'll need his help."

"Yes, I will. I want Ziyadah buried beside the statue at the head of the road. You know the one, Alec . . ."

"I know," he said, steadying her.

"My father would have wanted it that way."

"I guess so. Now we'd better go."

He felt the pressure of her hand as she answered, "Yes, we should. It's a long way back." There was no way of knowing whether she was conscious of the double meaning in her words.

"A long way," Alec repeated, taking her from the deep shadows of the mountain into the burnished silver light of early morning.

23 BLACK FLAME

María carefully lowered her big frame into her plane seat and had trouble getting the safety belt around her. Finally accomplishing it, she looked across at Alec and said, "Now he has a bad cold. He is like a baby always."

Alec glanced at the closed cabin door. Angel González and his copilot had two engines turning over. A third coughed and took hold. One more to go.

Henry had his seat belt fastened. He was looking out the window at Abd-al-Rahman and Tabari, who were standing beside their carriage. The Sheikh was waving but Henry didn't wave back.

"I guess you don't need to tell me more if you don't want to," he said to Alec. "But what does she do now?"

"She'll tell him after we're gone," Alec answered.

"How do you know?"

"I know *her*."

"I thought you said you had trouble reading her mind."

"That was before she lost Ziyadah."

"That makes everything all right?"

"No, just easier for me to understand how she feels."

"Maybe if I'd seen him . . ."

"It's better that you didn't," Alec said. "Now you have nothing to remember."

"As you do?"

Alec nodded. "As she does too," he said quietly.

The fourth engine caught, and Alec glanced nervously at the Black in his boxed stall. The stallion was alert to the loud noise but didn't seem to be unduly disturbed by it.

Henry said, "Abu Ishak was a *noble* desert chieftain and she was his daughter. I don't get it."

"He was also a good hater."

"What makes you say that?" Henry asked.

Alec smiled at María, who had unsnapped her seat belt momentarily to take a deep breath. "He had a lot of blood feuds that lasted for years."

"That's not unusual in the desert."

"That's exactly what I mean," Alec said.

The plane's wheels began to turn. Through the windows they could see Abd-al-Rahman with his arm around Tabari. No one could have met them without liking them. As hosts they were warm-hearted, cordial and hospitable, characteristics for which their race had always been known.

"What have blood feuds to do with it?" Henry asked.

"Only that the thirst for revenge comes easily to a race whose people have waged a perpetual war against each other for thousands of years."

"I suppose so," Henry agreed. "And besides, family feeling is very strong."

"Doesn't that make it easier to understand why she sought the Black's death in return for her father's life?" Alec asked.

"No," Henry said, "but it helps a little. Do you think she has any regrets for what she did?" The plane was picking up speed but they could still see the two young Arabs standing beside the carriage.

"Yes, I'm sure of it," Alec answered. "Taking Ziyadah's life with her own hand destroyed all her passion for revenge. If you'd seen her when she found him you'd know what I mean. She'll never be the same again."

"And she still has to tell her husband what happened," Henry said, grunting. "I'd like to be around."

"I wouldn't. He's touchy and he's lost Ziyadah."

"He's also in love," Henry added wisely.

They didn't speak again until they were airborne.

"Where are we going, Henry . . . home?"

"A race track would be nice and clean and simple after this. Got any suggestions?" The trainer picked up a Spanish newspaper from the seat beside him and tried to read it.

"No," Alec answered, "not now."

The big plane banked above the first peaks and slid back along the hanging plateau. For the next few minutes Alec looked down upon the massive house he had recently left and the patchwork of green fields and stone walls.

Then he heard Henry speak. "Here's a fine looking race horse. What'd he do, anyway?" The trainer meant his question for María, and he handed the newspaper to her.

Alec watched her take the paper in her big, fumbling hands. Her concern was for the health of Angel Rafael González, and she glanced only casually at the picture and caption.

"Señor, he is not one of ours. He has won a big race in Cuba."

"Is that right now? What's his name an' who owns him?"

She turned to the picture caption again, her small head cocked to one side as she read, "I believe . . . sí, it is *Flame*. There is no one owning him."

"No one owns him?"

"No one. It is the truth. It says so in the paper."

"Who picked up the purse money then?"

"*No one*, I repeat, Señor!" she answered in a fit of anger. "*Es verdad!* Read it for yourself if you do not believe me," she said, handing the newspaper back to Henry.

Henry said soothingly, "Now, María, I didn't mean to get you all upset."

She was watching the closed cabin door and wasn't listening to him. "Always the baby," she murmured. "He gives me no peace."

"But, please, María," Henry said insistently, going to her. "Who's the jock?"

"Jock?" she asked. "Jock? Who's a jock?" Her bright gaze shifted to Alec. *"Es loco!"* she called to him in a high-pitched voice, placing a finger on her temple.

Henry said patiently, "The rider, I mean. See, here he is, María, right up on the horse. They've got to give him a name."

She snatched the paper from his hands, reading the caption again. "No name," she said finally. "No one knows nothing, *nada*!" She flung her arms high in the air and the paper went flying. "They all went *pooph* after the race, even the horse! No one knows where they went. You understand, Señor, *entiende*? No one knows!"

"Go on," Henry said unbelievingly, "you're kiddin'."

María turned again to Alec, her finger beating a steady rhythm against her right temple.

Alec picked up the newspaper from where it had landed at his feet. The plane dropped into an air pocket, then steadied.

Henry said, "Thanks, María. I guess I don't want to hear any more of it, anyway. We've had our share of mysteries, heh, Alec?" he asked, turning to the boy.

Alec nodded without taking his eyes from the

paper. The Black appeared to be looking at the same picture, for suddenly his nostrils flared and he snorted at the picture of the giant, red horse named *Flame*.